THOUSAND
WORDS

JENNIFER BROWN

Little, Brown and Company
New York Boston

Copyright © 2013 by Jennifer Brown

Little, Brown and Company

Hachette Book Group
237 Park Avenue, New York, NY 10017
Visit our website at www.lb-teens.com

Little, Brown and Company is a division of Hachette Book Group, Inc.
The Little, Brown name and logo are trademarks of Hachette Book Group, Inc.

The publisher is not responsible for websites (or their content) that are not owned by the publisher.

First Edition: May 2013

Library of Congress Cataloging-in-Publication Data

Brown, Jennifer, 1972–
Thousand words / Jennifer Brown. — 1st ed.
p. cm.
Summary: Talked into sending a nude picture of herself to her boyfriend while she was drunk, Ashleigh became the center of a sexting scandal and is now in court-ordered community service, where she finds an unlikely ally, Mack.
ISBN 978-0-316-20972-4
[1. Community service (Punishment)—Fiction.   2. Sexting—Fiction.   3. Interpersonal relations—Fiction.   4. Dating (Social customs)—Fiction.   5. Conduct of life—Fiction.]   I. Title.
PZ7.B814224Tho 2013
[Fic]—dc23

2012029854

10 9 8 7 6 5 4 3 2 1

RRD-C

Printed in the United States of America

For Scott

COMMUNITY SERVICE

The community service I'd been court ordered to complete was held in one of the downstairs classrooms at the Chesterton Public Schools Central Office. Central Office, where my dad worked and where I'd spent many afternoons hanging out after school waiting for a ride home, would now be the place where I'd get a daily reminder that I'd massively messed up.

I walked the mile and a half from school, hoping the fresh October air would relax me, help shake out my nerves. It didn't work. I still had no idea what to expect and could only imagine myself locked in a painted-cinder-block room in the basement, something that looked a lot like the juvenile detention center where I'd learned, back in September, that big trouble was headed my way.

Sixty hours. Sixty impossibly long hours of community

service to pay for a crime that I hadn't even known I was committing when I committed it.

Sixty hours of being in the same room with people who were real criminals, who'd probably done things like sell drugs to children on playgrounds or steal money from cash registers; nothing like I'd done. Real criminals who would most likely take one look at me and eat me alive.

I wasn't sure if I had sixty hours in me.

But the court said I had to, so I walked to my fate, sucking in deep breaths until I was dizzy, and shaking my hands out until my fingertips tingled.

Mom had told me that morning to catch a ride home with Dad after community service, and I was nervous about that, too. Dad and I hadn't been alone in a room together, much less in a car together, since the whole mess started. Dad wasn't doing a lot of talking anymore, but he didn't need to do a lot of talking for me to know what he currently thought of me. My face burned with embarrassment every time I had to pass through a room he was occupying.

When I got to Central Office, I snuck back behind the receptionist's desk and into the inner offices where Dad and other personnel worked, wandering through just as I'd done a million times before. I could see Dad in his office, his face bathed by the blue glow of his computer screen, a phone planted against his ear. He was nodding and kept repeating, "Right, right," but if he saw me he made no show of it. I thought about waiting around for him to get off the phone so I could wave to him or say hi or do something to try to break through the barrier that jutted between us, but decided it was probably best not to make a spectacle of myself, especially given why I was there. I made my way back out to the main foyer and headed downstairs.

All the lights had been turned off, so the corridor was dark, but a rectangle of fluorescent light spilled through an open doorway at the end of the hall. I could hear voices coming out of that doorway. Room 104—the room I was supposed to report to. I walked toward it, reminding myself that I had been equally nervous going back to school that morning and I had weathered the day just fine. I paused at the doorway, took another deep breath, and stepped inside.

"... him to get his ass out of bed or he'd be goin' back to jail," a skinny blond girl with a big, pregnant belly and feather earrings was saying. She was bent over a piece of paper, carefully coloring something with a marker and talking to a woman who was standing by her table. The woman was nodding as if to agree with the girl, but when the girl glanced at me, the woman turned in my direction.

She had on black pants and a black jacket with a white dress shirt underneath. Her hair was super-curly and stuck out around her head in pomade-laden chunks. Her lipstick was a deep, dark red and her lips full and pouty.

"Hello," she said, all stiff and businesslike, walking toward me. "You must be Ashleigh Maynard."

I nodded.

She held out her hand. "I'm Mrs. Mosely. I oversee the Teens Talking program. You're here for community service hours, correct?"

I nodded again, putting my backpack down on a desk and digging through it until I found the piece of paper I was supposed to give her. She would have to sign it every day I worked, until I'd satisfied my hours, and then I was to turn it in to Tina, my lawyer, who would make sure it got filed with the court. The paper was all that stood between me and putting everything behind me. And I was more than ready to put everything behind me. Even if sixty hours seemed like such a long time. A lifetime.

The blond girl assessed me quickly, then went back to her coloring, shaking her head as if I'd done something despicable by walking into the room. I ignored her and turned my attention to Mrs. Mosely.

She took the paper and laid it on her desk, then turned and leaned back against the wooden desktop, crossing her arms over her chest.

"So you're to create some literature about texting, is that correct?" she asked.

"Yeah."

The blond girl made a low "oooh" sound, but Mrs. Mosely acted like she didn't hear it. I whipped my head around to glare at the girl.

There were two knocks on the doorframe and a guy I recognized from school popped into the room. He was wearing black jeans, way too big for him, and a leather jacket. He had a pair of headphones hanging around his neck like DJs do, and was carrying a comb in one hand.

"Yo, Mrs. Mose," he said. "What's up?" He tossed a paper that looked like mine onto Mrs. Mosely's desk as he walked by.

Another boy followed him in, very large, very quiet. He said nothing. Just headed over to a computer cubby in the back of the room. He dug some earbuds out of his pocket with his big, hammy hands and sat down.

"Hey, Darrell," Mrs. Mosely said. Then louder, "Hey, Mack." But the big kid in the back simply lifted his chin once in response, stuffing the earbuds into his ears and clicking the computer mouse diligently. Another girl walked in, her jeans so tight they cut into her belly, which wobbled behind an equally tight shirt with every step she took. She sat down next to the blonde.

"Hi, Mrs. Mosely," she said. "Wait till you hear what my moms said this morning about that thing we were talking about yesterday."

Mrs. Mosely held her finger up in a "wait" position, then turned back to me. "You'll probably want to start on the computer," she said. "Get some facts. Some statistics. Are you good at doing research?"

I nodded, thinking about how I used to be good at a lot of things. Before. Good at school. Good at cross-country. Good at making friends. Good to Kaleb.

Now what was I good at? Hiding from crowds? Ignoring catcalls? Staring down disgusting-minded jerks? Apologizing?

"Okay, excellent. Read news stories. Read blogs. Everything you can get your hands on. If a website exists that talks about it, I want you to know about that website and read it. That should take you at least a couple of weeks, okay? You will not be done researching in a day, so don't try to convince me that you are. You need to be armed with information. By the end of this, you will be an expert. As you may or may not know, you're going to be creating resources for schools. Posters, booklets, that kind of thing."

Before being assigned to work for Teens Talking, I'd already been familiar with the program. I remembered getting Teens Talking stuff when I was in junior high. Pamphlets about drugs or gangs or bullying or reckless driving or weapons. I never really read them. Just saw them on the guidance office's literature rack or received one in an assembly here or a seminar there. I'd always assumed they were written by people who worked in my dad's office or by the school psychologist. I never knew it was offenders writing them. And I certainly never would have guessed that I would someday be one of those offenders.

Mrs. Mosely continued. "We need these resources to be factual and reliable, so accuracy is important. When you're done gathering facts, you can start writing a rough draft. I'll proofread it. And then when it's all good to go, you can start creating the layout of your pamphlet or poster or PSA or whatever it is you decide to design. You can do some of the artwork yourself, like Kenzie is here, or you can design it all on the computer. After you're done with that, we'll look it all over to make sure it's ready to print. By then you should have your hours. Okay?" She leaned over her desk and signed my paper, then handed it back to me.

"Okay," I said, taking the paper, but my head was swimming and I wanted to go home. I could feel the girls' eyes on me, and even though Darrell never gave me more than a passing glance, I was sure he knew what had happened with me, because he went to school at Chesterton High. He'd probably seen the picture that had landed me in community service, maybe even had it on his phone right now, and that made me really uncomfortable. I'd hoped to at least get away from the constant feeling of humiliation here.

Mrs. Mosely cut into my thoughts. "Everyone in this group is on a different timetable, so it's not a race. Kenzie and Amber have both finished their research and writing and are down to creating artwork now. Darrell is in the writing stage. Mack is busy on the computer. And where's Angel?" she asked the room at large.

"I heard she got arrested," Amber said.

"Nah, man, she's just skippin' out," Darrell said. "I saw her over at Manny's house last night."

"What were you doing over there?" Mrs. Mosely asked, looking stern. Darrell laughed like what she'd said was a big joke. He gazed back down at his paper, shaking his head.

"Yo, Mose, how you get the word 'violence' if there ain't no 'i' in it?" he called out.

"It has an 'i,' stupid," Kenzie said. She and Amber shared a giggle.

Mrs. Mosely pretended she hadn't heard Kenzie's comment, or their laughs, and walked over to Darrell's desk. She pointed to the paper. "It has an 'i.' See? Right here before the 'o.'"

I took that as my cue and went over to the bank of computers in the back corner. I sat at the one next to the big guy Mrs. Mosely had called Mack. His finger was clicking the mouse rapidly. I wanted to get done so I could go home and curl up under my blankets and sleep. Today had been so tiring, and tomorrow promised to be just as emotionally wrenching. Every day would be, until all this—the name-calling and teasing, the catching up on schoolwork I'd missed, the community service, the wondering if I was still friends with Vonnie, the worrying about the board meeting that could be the end of my dad's career—blew over.

I logged on to the computer and got online, feeling a little more in my comfort zone than I'd expected. I'd done a ton of research papers for my AP English class, so in a way, community service didn't seem all that different from school. The very thought brought tears to my eyes. I had gone from researching English papers to writing community service warning pamphlets alongside a guy who couldn't spell "violence," even though I was pretty sure violence was exactly why Darrell was in here.

Before I became the subject of all the gossip at Chesterton High School, there was a rumor that Darrell had beat up his stepdad pretty badly; the guy had supposedly spent a week in the hospital with his jaw wired shut and a collapsed lung, and Darrell was lucky that all he got was some time in juvie followed by community service. If his stepdad had died, it could have been a lot worse. But anything Darrell had done was nowhere near as juicy as what I had done.

I bit my lip and tried not to think about it as I typed in the words "sexting and teens" and hit "search." Articles popped up, one after another, and I groaned inwardly.

Most of them were about me.

AUGUST

Message 1
OMG Ash what are you thinking?!

Vonnie's annual end-of-summer parties were legendary. The kind people were still talking about in December. The kind where someone spends three hours on hands and knees in the grass looking for lost car keys, the diving board gets broken, and somehow—though nobody will admit to doing it—the pool water is pranked with a grocery bag full of blue Jell-O powder.

I never missed Vonnie's parties. Even if she hadn't been my best friend since sixth grade, I still wouldn't have missed them. Her parties were where all the best stories were born, and where everybody who was anybody hung out.

But when I got there this year I wasn't exactly in the partying mood, partly because Coach Igo had decided summer break was officially over for cross-country athletes and had practically killed us doing hill runs in what felt like an oven pushed up to a thousand degrees. But I had other reasons for not really feeling like partying.

"You're late," Rachel Wellby said as soon as I walked through the front door. Rachel was Vonnie's friend from the volleyball team, and while I knew her from hanging out with Vonnie, there was something about Rachel I didn't really like all that much. She had an underlying air of bitchy competitiveness, especially when it came to my relationship with Vonnie. I always felt like Rachel didn't care for me, either, even though I never exactly knew why, and like she'd be thrilled if Vonnie decided to one day dump me. Honestly, I didn't get why Vonnie was such good friends with her, but it didn't matter. Vonnie was friends with a lot of people. I didn't own her.

Rachel was swaying in front of me, her wet swimsuit dripping in the entryway, a chlorinated puddle forming on the very expensive-looking throw rug. I could practically hear Vonnie's mom shouting all the way from their Cancún timeshare that the rug had been handwoven by an elderly craftsman they'd stumbled across in a little village in some foreign country I couldn't pronounce and that he'd died exactly nineteen minutes after weaving it and she could never get her memories of that amazing trip replaced, so get your wet clothes off it. "We're practically already sunburned,"

Rachel slurred. "And you missed the pizza. I don't think there's any left."

"Trust me, I know I'm late," I mumbled. My skin felt so hot I thought if I looked down I might see steam rising from my legs. The scent of the pool on Rachel made me all the more antsy to get into the water. I kicked off my shoes and rooted around in my gym bag for my bikini. "And I'm already sunburned, thanks to Coach Igo's love of torture."

"Whoa, somebody's crabby," Rachel said, then singsonged, "Don't worry. Kaleb will make you smile again."

"I don't think so," I said. "He's got a game."

This was the real reason I was cranky. Not because of an exhausting run, but because instead of dancing or drinking or floating lazily on a raft with my boyfriend, I was going to be doing those things alone. And this definitely wasn't the first time. It seemed like I'd been doing everything alone all summer.

Kaleb had been playing on a baseball team in a neighborhood league for something like twelve years. The guys on the team were like brothers. They did everything together. And this was their last summer on the field. Josh was going off to the marines in two weeks. Carlos was heading to some private college in Illinois. Daniel had started his new job a month earlier, and he never had time for anything anymore. And Jake, in a total surprise move, had shown up one day with a one-way ticket to Amsterdam and a plan to stay over there until he'd hooked up with enough sexy European girls to make him forget Katie, who'd broken up with him the last day of senior year.

I need to hang with my boys, Ash, Kaleb had told me when I suggested he blow them off for the most epic pool party of the summer. *I only have a few more weeks with them.*

But you only have a few more weeks with me, too, I'd argued.

No way. I have you forever.

Kaleb was exactly the kind of guy I'd want to have forever with. And I really wished I could believe him when he said stuff like that. I used to. At one time it really felt like forever might happen for us. But somehow we didn't feel so foreverish anymore. We felt temporary and dramatic and like we were always away from each other.

What seemed like forever was how long he'd been choosing his "boys" over me. All summer I'd practically had to beg for alone time with him before he went to college. In a few days he would be living four hours away. I'd be stuck at Chesterton High to finish up what were likely going to be the slowest two years of my life, and he would be partying with God-knew-how-many girls. College girls. Girls who would be impressed by his athletic build and his academic scholarship. Girls who were more ready for forever than any high school junior could ever be.

I continued pawing through my gym bag, trying to shake my irritation and my crummy boyfriend situation so I could have fun like everyone else at the party. I glanced up at

Rachel, but laughter in the kitchen had caught her attention and she'd already turned to follow it, giggling before she even knew what was so funny. Typical. I was surprised she'd stuck through a conversation with me as long as she had.

I located my swimsuit and trudged to the downstairs bathroom to change. I peeled off my smelly running clothes, threw on my suit, then made a beeline for the pool out back.

Vonnie was sprawled backward on a chaise lounge, her feet propped on the reclined back, her head lying where her feet should have been. One hand trailed off the edge of the lounge, her fingers delicately tracing the lip of a red plastic cup. Cheyenne and Annie sat on towels next to her. Cheyenne played with strands of Vonnie's hair, braiding them into teeny wet braids that would probably take ages to undo later.

"You should take your sunglasses off," I said, plopping onto the empty chaise next to Vonnie's. "You're going to get a tan line."

She turned her head to look at me, and after a couple of seconds, registered who I was. "Ashleigh!" she squealed, sitting up and throwing her arms drunkenly around my neck. "You came!"

I laughed—as if I'd ever not come—hugged her, then was practically pulled onto the ground when she flopped back onto the chaise. "Sorry I'm late," I said, trying to untangle myself from her hug. "Run went long. Igo about killed us today." I picked up her drink and took a swig. It was warm, and the sweetness made my jaws ache.

She waved her hand in front of her nose. "Phew! So I

smell!" She and the other girls burst into laughter; then she flipped over onto her stomach and called, "Stephen! Ashleigh needs the same treatment you gave me earlier!"

I had no idea what she was talking about, but after a second, Stephen Fillman and his friend Cody, both of whom had graduated last year with big-time football scholarships to state universities, pulled themselves out of the deep end and loped toward me, rivers of water coursing down their hairy legs and off their trunks and landing with loud splats on the concrete pool deck.

"No!" I squealed as Stephen bent over and wrapped my kicking feet into the crook of his arm. Cody came around the lounge and grabbed me by the waist. "Stop!" I yelled, gasping at how cold the water dripping off them felt on my skin. I playfully smacked at Cody's hands. I dropped Vonnie's cup on the pool deck, heard her curse and yell, "You owe me a drink, woman!," but I honestly couldn't even really register the words because the boys were carrying me and then swinging me in arcs over the deep end of the pool before letting go.

I free-fell into water so crisp and cold it startled me. I blew bubbles through my nose as soon as my head went under, letting the water caress my limbs and pull me down to the painted pool floor. My hair drifted around my face and I waved my arms, slow and dreamlike, then found the floor with my feet and pushed myself back up toward the sky, which looked impossibly blue filtered through the water.

I came up sputtering and laughing, feeling weightless,

like any worries, any fears, anything heavy I might have been holding on to were sliding off me and collecting on the bottom of the pool like silt.

It was the last moment I would feel that way for a long time.

Message 7
have u seen the txt that's been goin round by
chance? if not u better look.

As the sun started to go down, someone suggested a game of pool volleyball. I played on the boys' team: a bunch of football players and runners, most of whom had been drinking pretty heavily for a while, versus a rotation of girls from our state-title-winning girls' volleyball team. The guys needed me—the girls were killing us.

But we didn't care. It was fun losing. Adam took a spike directly to the head, twice, and we all laughed while he made the culprit, Cheyenne, kiss it. I sat on Stephen's shoulders to get the high shots. Vonnie had cranked up the stereo inside the house, setting the speakers in the open back door, and the game took on a rhythm that matched the music.

Everything felt different at this year's party. We were all older now. We were upperclassmen. Masters of our own destinies. We could do this. We could handle whatever came our way.

But then Rachel's new acrylic was ripped off. There was blood dripping from her finger into the water, which grossed Vonnie out and caused her to start gagging, and Rachel was making a huge wailing deal out of it. She staggered to the upstairs bathroom and the game broke up, everyone wrapping themselves in their towels or pillaging the kitchen cabinets for snacks or showing off on the diving board.

Cheyenne and Annie and a bunch of the guys tossed around a Frisbee that one of them found in the crawl space under the deck, and someone had lit the tiki torches that lined the patio. I found myself stretched out on the chaise next to Vonnie's again. She still had her sunglasses on, though the sun had gone down. Her hand had knocked over the fresh drink she'd poured for herself and she hadn't even noticed that the pink puddle was stretching toward the pool's edge.

"I think Stephen's into you," she said after a while.

I took a sip of a drink Cody had poured me earlier and made a face. "What are you talking about? No he's not." My mouth felt numb and I found myself laughing at everything, which was so annoying and I knew it, but I couldn't help it. This was the best I'd felt all day; maybe all summer.

I wished Kaleb had come with me. It would've been nice to have a good time with him for once.

Vonnie sat up. "Yes he is. He was totally rubbing your legs during that game."

"He was holding on to me. I would've fallen off," I said. She leaned forward and slid her sunglasses down her nose, staring at me over the top of them cynically. We both cracked up. "Okay, maybe," I said. "But I'm not interested. Remember Kaleb?"

Vonnie pulled off her glasses and rolled her eyes. "Who isn't here, by the way. Just in case you didn't notice." Vonnie hadn't had a boyfriend since Russell Hayes broke her heart last summer. She'd said she was swearing off teen romance and would wait for the real thing somewhere down the road when guys started maturing. In the meantime, her idea of a committed relationship was whatever relationship was available at the moment. Earlier I would have bet there was a good chance Vonnie was going to strike up a "relationship" with Stephen that night, so why she was grilling me about him when she knew I was dating Kaleb was beyond me.

"He had a baseball game."

"Which is interesting, given he's not actually on a baseball team."

"Von, I told you, it's an informal league. They've been playing forever. And everyone's—"

"I know, I know." She recited in a bored voice, "Everybody's splitting up because half of them are going away and the other half are stuck at Chesterton and it's going to be all sad and horrible because he won't get to see them again for a really long time." She turned toward me, her face serious. "But what about you, Buttercup?"

I smiled at the nickname Vonnie had been calling me ever since fourth grade, when we'd gone through a phase of being obsessed with the song "Build Me Up Buttercup." "I'm here, aren't I?" I took another swig and gazed at my pruny toes. The nail polish I'd put on the day before was all chipped and ugly, but I felt too floppy and relaxed to do anything about it.

"Of course you are. I didn't mean that." She leaned over to put her head on my shoulder, but the gap between our chairs was too wide, and her chair tipped sideways, spilling her onto the concrete. She laughed, her fingers digging into my arm. "I sat in my drink," she giggled, feeling the puddle under her butt with her other hand.

"Ow, you're shredding my arm, cat lady," I said, barely feeling her grip and laughing too hard to care.

Rachel came out of the house, dressed in street clothes, her finger wrapped in a huge bandage. She righted Vonnie's chaise and sat in it, leaving Vonnie on the ground between the two lounges. Rachel eyed us with a frown.

"She is messed up," Rachel said, as if she hadn't been equally messed up before the Great Nail Calamity.

"I am not," Vonnie said, letting go of my arm and lying back on the concrete. She waved her hand at Rachel dismissively. "I'm concerned for my best friend. What kind of friend would I be if I didn't worry about my best friend?"

"Why, what's up with you?" Rachel asked me.

"Nothing," I said, exasperation creeping into my voice. "Everything is fine. She's worrying for no reason."

Vonnie held up one finger drunkenly. "Reason. She's passing up the chance to be with Stephen because she's in love with a guy who isn't even here."

"You and Stephen?" Rachel said, her eyes getting big.

"No!" I said. "There is no me and Stephen. I'm with Kaleb."

"No you're not," Vonnie said. "You're here, and Kaleb is with his baseball team. Because he doesn't want to forget *them*." I got what she was saying. I had thought the same thing many times over the past few months. It seemed like I was always alone, only seeing Kaleb from a lawn chair out in a field somewhere. I might get a wink from the dugout. I might get a little slap on the butt or quick hug after a game, while he was on his way to grab a burger with the team, never inviting me to go with him because it was "boys only."

He was going to miss *them*. He wanted to rack up all the face time he could with *them*. But was he going to miss me? He didn't seem the least bit concerned about that.

Vonnie was right. He was with them because he wanted to be. And I was here alone because of it. But I wasn't ready to admit out loud that Vonnie had a point. Partly because she didn't understand Kaleb the way I understood him. She didn't know how special he made me feel when we were alone together and how it was worth it in those moments to have been on the sidelines for so long. But I also partly didn't want to admit it out loud because Rachel was sitting right there and I didn't want Rachel involved in my personal life.

"It's not like that," I mumbled, bending forward to pick at the remaining polish on my toes. My hair felt sticky in the folds of my neck, and the after-pool feeling was gross and I just wanted to take a shower and go to bed. Between the swimming and the alcohol and the day's run, I was super-tired, and super-tired of talking about Kaleb. This conversation wasn't helping my mood any. "He won't forget me, either."

The song on the radio changed and we all sang along for a moment, watching Stephen and Cody scale the gazebo roof, Adam videotaping them on his phone and Rich chucking pool toys at them to knock them off. Then Rachel said, "You should send him a picture of yourself. To take with him."

"Trust me, he's got like a zillion pictures of me."

"No, I mean a...*picture*...of yourself," she said, her voice going low and whispery.

Vonnie gasped, scandalized. "Dooo it," she said.

It took a minute for me to understand what they were talking about. Why would they be so excited about me taking a picture of myself for my boyfriend to have at college?

Then it hit me.

Not just any picture.

"Naked?" I whispered.

They both nodded. "You totally should," Rachel said. They looked at each other and laughed.

"Do it," Vonnie repeated.

"Oh, okay," I said sarcastically, then when they continued to grin at me like they were totally serious, added, "Uh-uh. No way. You two are crazy."

"He'll remember you for sure then," Rachel said.

"He's going to remember me anyway," I said hotly. I could feel my face start to burn. "What is the deal with you guys? He's playing baseball. It's not like I need to be chained to him twenty-four seven."

"Come on." Rachel rolled her eyes at me as if I were acting like a difficult child. "It'll be a going-away present. I'll bet he'll totally stare at it all the time. It's not like anyone's going to know."

"And you look hot," Vonnie added. "Hey, Stephen, wouldn't Ashleigh look hot naked?" she yelled, then fell onto her back in wild laughter.

I squealed and turned away from the gazebo, avoiding Stephen's reaction. "Shut up, Vonnie!" I said, but I couldn't help laughing a little, too.

"What are you afraid of? That he won't like it?" Rachel said over Vonnie's laughter. "He's a guy. Trust me, he wants to see you naked."

Kaleb and I had gotten pretty close, but not yet that close. He'd seen me in a bikini plenty of times, but that was as naked as I'd ever been in front of him...or any other boy, for that matter. He'd never even pushed for it, but sometimes when we were making out, his hands would start roaming and I knew that if I'd offered to take off my clothes, he would've been really happy.

Now that I thought about it, maybe if I'd offered to take off my clothes every now and then I wouldn't be taking a backseat to his boys all the time. Maybe it would be me he'd be worried about missing so much.

"You know, he's going to be meeting tons of girls at college," Rachel said. "And they probably won't have any problem getting naked in front of him."

"That's right," Vonnie added. "You should be proactive." But she messed up the word and it came out more like *prorackive*.

"Thank you, guys," I said. "That makes me feel tons better. Really."

I didn't need them to point out that he was going to be around college girls. I was already a little worried about what kind of girls he would meet at college. They'd be older than me, and probably willing to do things I wasn't willing to do.

Maybe Rachel and Vonnie were right. Maybe it would be the going-away present he needed to get his mind off his boys and totally onto me. If I was going to compete with college girls, maybe I had to be willing to woman up a little. I couldn't be a baby forever.

"What am I supposed to…how would I even…?" I

laughed, covering my face with my hands. "I can't believe I'm talking about this right now."

"It's not rocket science. Just get naked, take a picture with your cell phone, and text it to him," Rachel said. "Totally easy."

Vonnie put her hand on my arm. "Oh! And just be like, 'See what you're missing? There's more where this came from.' He'll crap himself."

The music thumped, louder and louder. Everyone had gotten out of the pool and was milling around the patio, the flicker of the tiki flames bouncing off their bare skin, which looked soft and warm and tan. In that moment, it felt like summer would never end.

My head buzzed with the noise and my stomach twisted up in butterflies. I felt wired, like every nerve ending in my body was zapping into place.

"You guys, I can't," I whispered, but inside I was starting to think I could.

"Why not? I totally would," Rachel said, her voice dripping with derision, like I was the most infantile person she'd ever met. "My brother's girlfriend does it all the time. And she's in ninth grade."

"It would be a great way for you to show him how much you love him," Vonnie added sincerely. "Remind him you belong to him, you know?"

That was what I wanted. It was *all* I wanted, really. To let Kaleb know that while his boys were important, I was the real thing. I loved him. I was willing to give him something special. I didn't want him to forget me.

The song switched, then played out and switched again. Cheyenne and Annie came over and squeezed next to Rachel on the chaise. Vonnie and the other girls talked about how much they hated their coach, and a couple of older kids started showing up as it got later, barging through the gate with towels slung over their shoulders as if they owned the place. The party raged on, bumping with music and splashing and whoops. But I wasn't really there. I was in my own head, swimming in my thoughts, going round and round until I was dizzy and bold.

"I'm gonna do it," I said at last, and Vonnie and Rachel stared at me with wide eyes.

"What?" Cheyenne asked. "What's she gonna do?"

But I didn't answer. I gulped down the last of my drink and stood up. I could hear Rachel whispering to the other girls as I strode into the house. I didn't look back.

COMMUNITY SERVICE

We weren't required to work silently in community service, but I did anyway. Darrell and Amber and Kenzie all knew each other and shared stories that were funny or interesting or exciting or terrible only to them. I couldn't have added anything even if I'd wanted to.

Their conversations would go like this:

"Y'all hear Fat Benny got busted?"

"Who's that?"

"You know, Sanchez's stepbrother."

"You mean Mike?"

"No, his other stepbrother. The one with the red hair who passed out that jank acid at Ace's house that one time?"

"Oh, that guy. I thought he was dead."

"No, you're prolly thinking of Travis. Dude that crashed his motorcycle into the Big Burger."

"Oh, yeah, I remember that. Went right through the window."

On and on it would go, and I would try to follow the trail, finding myself sketching little family trees in my mind. And I'd think, *Oh, I remember when that guy drove through the Big Burger window. It was on the news.* It seemed surreal to me that I was hanging out with people who knew him personally, but I would never say anything because to me it was just another news story and to them it was something that had happened in their lives, and our experiences could never be the same.

Plus, I didn't want to open up any discussion about what might have been on the news about the sexting scandal at Chesterton High. I had a feeling I didn't want to know what they'd all seen about me.

So instead, I sat at my computer and did my research, trying to follow their conversations in fits and starts, and wondering what Mack was doing that required so much clicking and why he never got involved, either.

Mack had never spoken. At least not that I'd heard. I almost wondered if he could. What was weirder was that nobody really ever spoke to him, either. Not even Mrs. Mosely, other than to say hi when he walked in.

Mrs. Mosely spent most of her time bent over a book or would sometimes step out into the hallway to use her cell phone. Once, the front-desk receptionist came down and lingered outside our door until she got Mrs. Mosely's attention, and then they hung out in the hallway and talked for a while.

But every now and then someone would say something that would interest even Mrs. Mosely, and I would see her glance up from her book, sitting very still, her eyes darting back and forth between Darrell, Kenzie, and Amber, who never seemed to even notice that there was anyone else in the room with them.

"My mom is getting divorced again," Amber said as we settled into our work routines on my fourth day. "This is number five. I keep telling her to mess around with as many dudes as she wants, just stop marrying them, but she says she can't help it if she falls in love."

Kenzie leaned back in her chair and rubbed her belly. "Shit. Look what falling in love got me," she said. "Got me fat." And they both laughed.

There was silence for a few minutes, and then Darrell piped up from his computer. "You ever regret it? Sleeping with that Jonah guy, I mean?" Darrell was always doing that—asking people really awkward questions at really awkward times. Mrs. Mosely's head popped up and she studied Kenzie. I stopped reading and turned my head slightly, too, watching them out of the corner of my eye.

"No. You regret beating the shit out of people?" Kenzie's tone was hostile, but Darrell pressed his lips together, sheepish.

"Sometimes, yeah. Like when I see my mom cry, I do. I don't mean to make nobody cry. I got a hot head is all."

The room was silent and had an on-edge feel that couldn't be ignored. I waited for Mrs. Mosely to say something, but she just kept staring over the top of her book.

Then, finally, Amber cut the silence. "We all'd rather be out there having a good time than doing this, right? I regret stuff, too. Lots of stuff. Especially stuff that got me here every day. Nothing wrong with regret."

"Well, I don't regret anything," Kenzie said. "Life's too short for that shit." She pushed away from her desk and pulled herself to standing, her hand on the small of her back. "Mrs. Mosely, can I use the restroom, please? Baby's sitting down low."

Restroom breaks were supposed to be scheduled, and Mosely didn't often veer from the schedule. But this time she nodded, and watched Kenzie saunter out of the classroom before finally looking back at her book.

"Everybody regrets some things," Darrell muttered after Kenzie had left. "Wouldn't be human not to."

And that was the end of the conversation. But for some reason I couldn't turn my eyes back to the article I'd been reading. I knew it was full of things I regretted. Things I regretted so much it hurt to even look at them, to remember them. I squeezed my eyes shut tight. I had so many regrets, I wasn't even sure where they began. Was my biggest regret not having the guts to tell Rachel to take a hike? Was it falling in love with Kaleb? Or was it the simple motion of standing up, tossing a drink, and marching into Vonnie's house that night at the pool party?

Or was it something else altogether? Something deeper, more ingrained in me?

I opened my eyes and glanced to my left. Mack had stopped clicking and was staring right at me. Even though his earbuds were in, I was sure he'd heard everything they'd all said. And for some reason, I had a feeling he knew why I was so silent. Our eyes locked for the briefest moment before he turned back to his computer.

AUGUST

Message 13
uh i don't think u ment to send this to me lol

Only a few partiers were inside Vonnie's house, and they
were all in the kitchen, easy to slip past as I charged toward
my things. If even one of them had stopped me to talk, I
probably would have lost the resolve I'd worked up out on
the pool deck. My stomach felt full of butterflies, and I
actually giggled to myself as I located my bag by the front
door and rooted through it for my cell phone.

I grabbed the phone and bag and ran downstairs, notic-
ing how grainy everything looked. I felt removed from my
surroundings, like they were movie props and I was watching them go by in someone else's life.

There was a tiny voice in the back of my mind wondering if I was really going to do this. I was an honor student. An athlete. I made dinner with my parents every night and I got awards and I was a virgin. I rarely drank, I was responsible, I was not the kind of person who normally did something like this.

But what did that mean, *something like this*? It's not like this was a huge deal. People did it all the time. It was just for fun. Who would it really hurt?

Locked inside the bathroom, I turned on the light and shed my bikini, then faced the mirror, immediately feeling really stupid. There was no way I could actually take this picture. What if he didn't like it? What if he got mad at me for sending it? What if he thought I looked ugly?

My breasts were way too small—one of those athletic chests boys are always complaining about. My hair was in nasty, half-dried ropes, and my eyes were red from the chlorine. I closed them and took a deep breath, straightening my thoughts.

I was not ugly. Kaleb would never think I was ugly. How many times had he told me he thought I was beautiful? Every time we talked, almost. I was just nervous. And nervous about what?

I opened my eyes and studied myself again.

At least I was tan. I worked out every day, so I was in good shape. And it's not as if anyone is perfect, right? And, seriously, like Rachel said, Kaleb was a guy. He was not going to be picky.

And he loved me. He would love this. He would love that we shared this.

I raked my fingers through my hair to break up some of the tangles, then held the phone in front of me and off to the side so everything was showing in the full-length mirror. I heard the music pounding outside and distant laughter and some squeals. A splash. The sound of something falling over with a clang in the kitchen. A car honk. I thought I could even hear the electricity buzzing in the lightbulbs. Or maybe the buzzing was coming from the adrenaline coursing through me. Vonnie and Rachel would never believe I'd done this.

"Just do it," I said aloud, and before I could give it any more thought, I struck a pose with my free arm draped over my head sexily, cocked one hip to the side, pooched my lips, and took the picture.

I turned the phone around and gazed at the screen. I was surprised to see that I didn't look as bad as I'd thought I might. My pose was good, and the wet hair gave the shot an even sexier vibe. My heart was pounding as I thumbed a message—WISH YOU WERE HERE XOXO—and hit Send. And then stood, holding my phone up against my stomach and staring at myself unbelievingly in the mirror.

I got dressed in my street clothes, feeling way too exposed in my bikini all of a sudden, and raced back up the stairs. I grabbed a glass of water on my way out to the patio. My throat felt parched and swollen, and my hands were definitely shaking.

As soon as Rachel and Vonnie saw me coming, their faces lit up with interest. Vonnie had moved to my lounge but scooted over and patted the plastic next to her. I could tell by the looks on Cheyenne's and Annie's faces that they'd been filled in on what I'd been doing inside.

"Well...?" Rachel said as I made my way over.

I nodded, biting my lower lip. "I did it."

They all gasped. "Shut up, you did?" Vonnie crowed.

I nodded again. "Full frontal."

"Oh my God, full frontal? Even my brother's slutty girlfriend only shows her boobs," Rachel said.

My face felt more on fire than it had during that morning's run. I snapped my fingers, diva-style, and jokingly gestured down the length of my body. "That's because your brother's slutty girlfriend doesn't have this," I said.

We all collapsed into laughter, the girls saying they couldn't believe it, they never thought I'd actually go through with it, they'd never have had the guts to do it, and holy crap, what was Kaleb going to say.

"Let me see it," Vonnie said, holding out her hand.

I gripped my phone tighter and whipped it behind my back. "No way!"

She rolled her eyes. "Come on, it's not like I've never seen you naked before. I'm not some kind of perv or anything. I just want to see how it came out."

I stuffed the phone in my front pocket, imagining what could happen if I gave it to Vonnie. I could see it now, my picture getting passed around the pool, Vonnie screeching to Stephen that he could see me naked if he was still curious. "Forget it. Nobody but Kaleb is ever going to see this. I'd die first."

"Oh, suddenly she gets all shy," Rachel commented, and I shot her a look. She raised her eyebrows at me. "I'm kidding! If it makes you feel any better, I definitely don't want to see it."

"Fine," Vonnie said. "But at least tell us about it."

I opened my mouth, but before I could speak a word, I was interrupted by my phone vibrating in my pocket. I'd gotten a text.

From Kaleb.

COMMUNITY SERVICE

On my sixth community service day, Amber was finished with her pamphlet, so Mrs. Mosely brought in some chips and cheese dip and sodas and mini doughnuts. Apparently, whenever someone finished a project in Teens Talking, it was treated like a small celebration. There was a presentation, and Mrs. Mosely asked questions, and then she broke out the food and everyone congratulated the person who was done with their time. That was the most important part to us—the proof that eventually your service would end and maybe your life would get back to normal. We were all simultaneously jealous of and motivated by Amber.

She showed up late, wearing a shiny black jumper that was at least two sizes too small for her, and a pair of heels. Her hair was piled up on top of her head like she was going to prom, and it occurred to me that probably Amber and Kenzie, and maybe some of these other guys, didn't even go to school anymore. Instead of planning for prom, they were here, writing pamphlets, doing their time, then going back to lives full of drugs and vandalism and pregnancy and things that never really entered my world. But no sooner did I have the thought than I realized I was probably making an unfair assessment. After all, I was there, wasn't I? It was my world now.

· Mrs. Mosely had us all pull our desks into a semicircle so everyone could see. Kenzie sat next to another girl who I assumed was Angel, the girl who'd been missing last week. Their heads were together, tucked low, as they whispered, every so often stifling laughter behind their hands. Kenzie absently rubbed her stomach with one hand the way pregnant women do. It seemed weird that in a few weeks, her hand would be cradling a baby's head instead; her whole life would be changed forever.

"Yo, Mose, I'm here, man," Darrell said, bouncing into the room at the last second. "Don't count me absent." Following close behind him was Mack, silent as ever, who slouched into the chair next to mine and stretched his legs in front of him, crossing them at the ankles.

"Better late than never, I suppose," Mrs. Mosely said, leaning back against her desk, arms folded across her chest. Darrell dropped his paper onto her desk and plopped into a chair on the other side of Angel, and we all settled down.

"Okay," Mrs. Mosely said, "as you all know, today is Amber's last day. She's completed her requirement and finished her project, which she's going to share with you momentarily." She glanced at Amber. Amber's cheeks flushed red, and she ducked her head down toward her desk, one leg bouncing nervously. "After Amber shares her project with us, we have some treats. You will take a five-minute break to get yourself a plate, and then everyone must get back to work, okay? This is not a social gathering." She gazed at us each in turn. I wondered if Mosely ever looked soft. I wondered if she went home at night and put on pink fuzzy pajama bottoms and brushed the pomade out of her hair and washed her makeup off and watched chick flicks. Somehow I doubted it.

"No problem," Darrell said.

"Okay. Remember to be polite. Your turn to do this will come soon enough."

"Yeah, and karma will bite y'all's asses if you mess with my girl," Kenzie said.

Mrs. Mosely took a breath, ignoring Kenzie, then nodded at Amber and sat down. Amber gathered up some papers and strode to the middle of the semicircle.

"So my project was about alcoholism because I got busted with Minor in Possession in my cousin's car. She got a DUI, though." She looked at Mrs. Mosely nervously, and Mrs. Mosely nodded for her to continue. "So basically I decided to make some posters that talk about alcoholism and how it's not cool to get wasted." Amber unrolled a poster of a kid partying, holding a glass of something high and proud, with the caption HE NEVER MADE IT HOME THAT NIGHT.

And then unrolled another of a girl in a hospital bed with all these tubes and wires coming out of her: WHEN PARTYING LEADS TO POISONING. And another of a little child crying: ALCOHOLISM DESTROYS FAMILIES. And finally one of a girl in a semiformal, her makeup smeared and her face red with tears, blotches of what looked like vomit staining the front of her dress: SHE WANTED TO LOOK SEXY FOR THE PARTY.

I thought the posters were all really professional-looking, but from some of the things I'd overheard Amber and Kenzie talk about, I guessed Amber didn't really believe in what the posters said, because she was still partying.

On the other hand, I couldn't help thinking that had I not been partying that night back in August, I wouldn't even have been sitting in room 104. I wanted to suggest to Amber that she should add another poster, one of a girl taking a photo of herself, captioned ALCOHOL DESTROYS REPUTATIONS.

I wanted to believe that the events of that night were what got me here. I wanted to think that if I hadn't been drinking or I hadn't listened to Rachel and Vonnie or I hadn't done any number of other things, this wouldn't have happened. But who knew for sure? Maybe I was just destined to live this misery.

Amber went on to read from a pamphlet she'd made, where she quoted statistics about teen alcoholism and deaths due to drinking, as well as some myths.

After she was done, she put the posters and pamphlet on Mrs. Mosely's desk and stood awkwardly in front of us. "Um, I wanted to say that I'm glad I had to do this project because I have a lot of uncles and cousins who are alcoholics and it has messed up our whole family. And I don't want to end up like them and I'm sort of afraid that I will."

Mrs. Mosely, who'd simply been watching with that stern look on her face throughout the whole presentation, let Amber's words sink in and then said, "Now that you know better, you can do better, right? You don't have to be like them. And hopefully you'll reach someone else with your posters and they can do better, too."

Amber wiped the corners of her eyes with her long manicured fingers and nodded.

Mrs. Mosely turned to face us. "Does anyone have any questions for Amber?"

Darrell raised his hand.

"Go ahead."

"I don't have a question," he said. "I liked the posters. They were really good. That chick in the pink dress was messed up. Still hot, though."

"All right, Darrell, thank you for that," Mrs. Mosely said in a tired voice. "Anyone else?"

Nobody spoke, so Mrs. Mosely stood, walked over, and wrapped her arm around Amber. "Let's congratulate Amber for finishing her community service." We all clapped. "We'll miss you, but we don't want to see you back here," she said. I guessed that was Mrs. Mosely's way of being sentimental. "Okay, five minutes starts now."

Everyone got up and moved toward the food table, except for Mrs. Mosely and Amber, who were rolling up the posters and snapping rubber bands around them, and Mack, who stayed in his chair, continuing to look straight ahead as if Amber were still showing her presentation.

I grabbed a plate and some chips and drizzled cheese dip over the top of them. My stomach growled.

I piled a few doughnuts on my plate and started to head toward my computer but almost ran into Kenzie and Angel, who stood behind me, their shoulders touching. Kenzie had a weird grin on her face.

"We know why you're here," she said. She licked some cheese dip off her finger. A little splat of it dripped and landed on her stomach, but she didn't seem to notice.

"Okay," I said, because I wasn't sure what I was supposed to say to something like that. But they didn't look away or move. I glared. "And your point is?"

"It would be funny if it wasn't so sad," she said. "Like you didn't get enough attention being all miss-perfect-got-money-athlete, you gotta go get more attention by sending crotch shots to everyone?"

My face burned at the word "crotch." "It wasn't a crotch shot. Don't be disgusting. And I didn't send it to anyone but my boyfriend," I said, then amended, "*Ex*-boyfriend."

Kenzie and Angel exchanged a glance. Kenzie looked amused, but Angel looked pissed.

"You're the disgusting one. Sending naked pictures to your ex-boyfriend?" Kenzie said. She laughed derisively. "God, how desperate! Even I'm not that desperate, and I got a baby coming."

"He was my boyfriend at the time," I said, as if it mattered. I could feel my fingers shaking and hear the little rattle my chips made as the plate shook, but I refused to back down. I didn't know what these girls were in community service for, but it definitely wasn't for being honor roll students. They had no room to talk. "Not that I need to explain it to you."

"I don't care about your boyfriend. What I care about is now *my* boyfriend has that picture on his computer," Angel said. "And I think that's what you wanted. Ho."

Of course, I knew that when a photo is uploaded onto a computer, anything can happen to it. It can float around forever, even if it's deleted off the original website it was put up on. I just didn't like to think about that. The thought made me nauseous. God only knew how many more people had it.

"You're nasty," Kenzie said, smirking at me over her plate of food.

I didn't know what to say. I was all apologized out, and even if I hadn't been, I sure as hell wasn't going to apologize to these two for something that had nothing to do with them. "That's your boyfriend and your problem," I finally said, and tried to move around them, but they shuffled a step sideways to block me. My hand holding the plate continued to shake, and I hoped they didn't notice.

I searched for something to say to get them to go away, but I didn't need to say anything, because before I could open my mouth, someone else did.

"Leave her alone."

The voice was loud and made everyone jump. Even Mrs.

Mosely and Amber looked up. The room got silent and all eyes turned to Mack, who still sat in his place in the semicircle. He didn't even acknowledge that anyone was looking at him.

Kenzie and Angel glared at him and then eventually turned back to me and glared at me, as if I'd had something to do with Mack speaking, but to my surprise they didn't say anything to either of us. After a few seconds, they sauntered off, back to their desks, moving their chairs out of the semicircle and sitting close to each other.

They were whispering again, but I did my best to ignore them, took a deep breath, and carried my plate to my space by the computer. My appetite was gone, and I wanted nothing more than to bolt out of there, but I supposed that Mrs. Mosely, and the court, would be less than willing to write off my community service if I hadn't done it.

I logged on to my computer and went back to researching, doing my best to put them out of my mind completely.

I'd plowed through most of the articles about me and had found some other stories of girls in situations similar to mine. One had even killed herself, the bullying had gotten so bad, and I found myself swallowing and swallowing while I read that story, hoping and praying that it didn't get that bad for me. Hoping and praying that I wouldn't one horrible day find myself wanting to end it all because someone had sought revenge for something I didn't even do. All because somebody's boyfriend or brother or husband had seen me naked. All because people were calling me names that didn't describe me and saying things about me that weren't true. All because people were hating on me on message boards and websites and in the comments fields of news stories.

My vision got blurry as I read through the articles. My throat felt dry and I wanted to go home. I didn't even notice that Mack had gotten up from the semicircle and slid into his usual chair right next to me, gobbling a mini-doughnut, his fingers repetitively clicking the mouse like always.

There was something about him that was mysterious, and kind of frightening, and clearly I wasn't the only one who felt it. Everyone had gone silent when he'd simply spoken three words earlier. Kenzie and Amber had laid right off me. They'd walked away. They were tough, and clearly they were afraid of Mack. I took him in, from his mess of greasy curls to his ripped denim jacket to his filthy fingernails and huge thighs spread out over the chair. He looked like he could kill a person—the kind of guy you'd cross the street to get away from if he was walking toward you on the sidewalk.

But there was something else about him, too. His eyes, maybe. How they'd looked at me the day of the conversation about regrets. They were bright and glossy, and his face was open and innocent. Under the bulk and the grease and the frowning, growling aura, he seemed...like he cared.

I reached over and touched his sleeve very lightly. "Thanks," I said. "For what you did earlier."

He didn't answer, but for a moment his finger stopped clicking the mouse. It was a pulse, a beat, of acknowledgment, and after the pulse, he continued chewing his mouthful of doughnut and went back to whatever he was clicking on.

AUGUST

Message 29
WTF?! Why would someone do that?! Ur stupid.

Kaleb and I met at the Halloween Ghoul Run 5K in the fall of my sophomore year. Per our team's tradition, all the guys had dressed in drag. Kaleb was in a blue party dress, the short skirt shifting up with each step, showing a pair of black running shorts underneath. He was wearing a long blond wig and lipstick, but the wig had fallen off somewhere around mile two. I'd been running behind him, a zombie marathon runner, and I bent to pick up his wig and then carried it to the end of the run.

I didn't know him very well. He was a senior and I was a sophomore, and even though Vonnie hung out with tons of seniors, I didn't have that same fearlessness. He seemed so much older. And incredibly athletic. His Adam's apple was prominent and his legs pure muscle, his hips small and square. I'd never seen him without a shirt on, but I guessed his abs were a six-pack.

So my legs quaked and I felt like such a little kid as I held the wig out to him at the water station a few feet past the finish line. Despite my stopping to pick up the wig, I'd finished only three strides behind him.

"Here," I said, gulping in air, my other hand on my hip.

He poured a cup of water over the top of his head, tossed the empty cup into the trash bin, and gazed at the wig as if he'd never seen it before. "Oh," he said after a minute, his hand reaching up to rub his wig-free head. "Thanks." He took the wig out of my hand and tossed it into the bin on top of the used water cup. A drop of water hung heavily on his eyelashes, and only then did I notice how clear and green his eyes were. I'd never been this close to him before. A sweaty, sunny smell radiated off of him. Something about the scent was a total turn-on. "I don't really need it anymore," he said. "I like your costume. Zombie. Cool."

I looked down at my ripped running pants, the T-shirt with tire tracks and dirt smudges clinging to my middle. "Thanks," I said. "I kind of copped out, though. I'm in running clothes. Got to be a lot harder to run in a dress."

He grinned. "It was kind of nice, actually. Breezy. I'm thinking about wearing it all the time. To our first meet, for sure."

He curtsied clumsily, and I couldn't help smiling.

"You will definitely be noticed if you do," I said.

Later, as I sat on a curb eating bagels with some girls I knew from the team, he came over and asked for my cell number. Said he liked to keep in touch with all the cross-country team members. Liked to have get-togethers and stuff. But there was something about the way he leaned over me as I wrote my first and last name down on the back of his hand with a red pen that made me feel like he wanted my number for a different reason. I was so giddy at the idea, I couldn't keep the flirty smile off my face.

He studied what I'd written. "Great. I'll text you later today, Ashleigh."

"Okay."

He paused. "You have a great smile." And then he jogged off to where some guys were hanging out over by a tent where they were selling pineapple wedges in cups.

And you have a great everything, I thought, and had to force myself not to get up and do a little jumpy dance.

He texted me that night, and pretty much every night after that. At first, we just talked about cross-country and running and meets. But after a while, we started talking about other things, too, like our families and what movies we liked. And then we started flirting a lot. Talking on the phone. Hanging out at school. We went out a few times. He kissed me in the back booth of a diner after a rough meet during which I'd rolled my ankle on a pinecone. We'd been practically inseparable ever since.

And it was perfect. During the school year, we hung out together all the time. We went to movies and played paintball and chilled at his friend Silas's house playing video games and eating greasy takeout. He met me at my locker between classes. He drove me to school and home again, and we made out in my empty house until Mom called to say she was leaving work and would be home shortly.

But then he graduated. And even though I tried to enjoy myself, to be happy for him, I couldn't help feeling like this was the beginning of the end for us. Which wouldn't be the end of the world, and I knew that. But it would *feel* kind of like the end of the world, anyway. I loved him.

But for a moment during Vonnie's end-of-summer party, the volleyball game over and Rachel's nail tragedy a thing of the past, Vonnie drunkenly giggling on her chaise lounge again and a naked photo of me winging its way through cyberspace toward my boyfriend...at least for that moment...I knew I had his full attention.

I knew I had something that his boys would never have. It felt powerful. And when my phone vibrated in my pocket minutes after I'd sent the photo, a jolt of excitement surged through me. He'd received it.

His text simply said: OMG.

And I didn't know how to answer that. I was too nervous and kind of embarrassed and a little drunk and hyped up, so I simply texted a smiley face and tucked the phone back into my pocket. The bugs were starting to get thick, so we migrated into Vonnie's house, and we started playing dumb junior high games like spin the bottle and truth or dare and I had to kiss Cheyenne's foot and someone dared Cody to run up to the highway and moon passing cars and it was all so hilariously stupid I kind of forgot about the picture I'd sent.

The morning after the party, I woke up to my phone vibrating in my pocket again. I rolled over and found myself nose to nose with Vonnie's yellow Lab, Starkey, on Vonnie's bedroom floor. My head was resting on my gym bag, which I'd at some point brought from the bathroom to her bedroom. My feet were pushed up against Rachel's stomach; she was crashed half-on and half-off Vonnie's beanbag chair. Vonnie and Cheyenne were squeezed into Vonnie's bed. Vonnie had one flip-flop on. Cheyenne was snoring.

I shimmied around so I could dig my phone out of my pocket and checked the screen. It was Kaleb.

LAKE 2DAY?

I groaned inwardly. I felt so waterlogged and beaten up from last night, all I wanted to do was sleep some more. But I missed him. I wanted to see him. I hardly ever got time with him, so no way would I turn down the chance to be with him.

YEP WHEN?

1 HR UR HOUSE

NO VON'S

OK

I rolled onto my back, slid my leg out from under

Rachel's gut, and stretched, rubbing my eyes and wishing I'd drunk some water before bed. At least I had my bikini with me, so I wouldn't need to go home first.

I blinked at the ceiling for a while, but when my eyes started drooping again, I forced myself to sit up, yawning. I sent my mom a text, telling her I was going to the lake with Kaleb and would be home later, and headed to Vonnie's bathroom for a shower.

I didn't need to ask. Vonnie's house was like my second home, and vice versa. During the summer, I would shower at Vonnie's house as often as I'd shower at my own. I could use her shampoo, her razor, everything. It was one of the great things about having a best friend like Vonnie. She didn't care about those kinds of things.

Mom texted me back—LET ME KNOW IF YOU'RE EATING DINNER WITH US—as I padded into the bathroom. I started the shower, shucked out of my clothes, and caught sight of myself in the mirror.

The mirror.

Oh my God.

My stomach dropped as the memory flooded back at me, faint and spotty like a movie I'd seen years ago and couldn't really remember. But I knew what I'd done. I'd sent Kaleb a picture of myself. Posing naked.

My eyes searched the mirror in disbelief. At once, I was fully awake.

I felt so vulnerable. But in a good way. If he liked it. Dear God, please let him have liked it. That picture must have really surprised him. And as much as I couldn't believe I'd done it, I was kind of excited about it, too.

I closed my eyes. Less than an hour. In less than an hour I'd see him.

I climbed into the shower, hoping more than anything that he'd liked what he'd seen. It never even occurred to me to think about anything else.

"So, you got anything on under there or you planning to swim naked?" Kaleb asked, pointing to the butter-yellow sundress I'd borrowed from Vonnie's closet.

I blushed. I could feel the blood rising up my face, making my ears hot. "You never know."

"Obviously not," he said, putting the truck into gear and pulling out of Vonnie's driveway, smiling. "You're full of surprises."

I could feel my whole body going warm. He seemed really happy, which was a huge relief. "You liked it?"

He glanced over at me with wide eyes. "You're kidding, right?"

"Well, I wasn't sure. Rachel and Von talked me into it."

He reached over and laced his fingers through mine. "Remind me to thank Rachel and Von."

A tingling sensation flooded me, part naughtiness, part relief. "I was nervous you'd get mad. Or would hate it."

He laughed. "Uh...mad was definitely not what I was feeling. More like I wanted to be there at the party instead of at the stupid pizza place with the team."

I grinned. Mission accomplished. I'd gotten his attention. I'd shown him that I had something to offer that his "boys" definitely did not have. I imagined him sitting around a sticky table, all those sweaty guys chewing with their mouths open and saying stupid things, and then his phone buzzing with a text. A text he'd never expected. I pictured his eyebrows shooting up, and him unable to swallow his pizza. I imagined a secret smile sliding slowly across his face and, in my mind's eye, when one of his boys noticed it, Kaleb said, *Nothing, just a text from Ashleigh.* I liked picturing this happening. In a way it was as if I'd stolen a moment with him when I wasn't supposed to.

"I looked at it about a thousand times last night," he said. "You really blew me away." Exactly what I wanted.

We drove in silence for a while, our hands wrapped around each other's so tightly our palms were sweating. We filled a cooler with sodas and sandwiches, then stopped at his uncle's house on the way to the lake to borrow his boat. We spent the day on the water, hanging out, soaking up sun, and swimming. I laid out across the front of the boat, and Kaleb stared at me in a way he never had before, and when we stopped in the shade of a secluded cove to eat lunch, our sandwiches and sodas grew warm as we kissed each other instead, our limbs tangled together, his hands searching around and under my bikini. "You're so beautiful," he whispered into my hair. "You shouldn't have sent me that picture."

I stopped, pulled back from him. "Why?"

He grinned, then bent and kissed my collarbone. "Because it only made me want you all the more now. It's not fair to show me something I can't have."

I fake pouted. "Poor baby. But you can have this." And I pulled him to me for a long, slow kiss.

Afterward, he nuzzled his face into my neck and breathed deep, sprinkling kisses all down my shoulders and chest, right up to my bikini top. He rested his chin on my chest and gazed up at me with his intense eyes. "You don't have to send me photos like that, Ashleigh. I want to be with you anyway."

I ran my fingers through his hair. "That's exactly why I sent it, though," I said. "I want to be with you, too. I wanted to show you that."

"Yeah, but what if it got out somehow? I'd have to kick the ass of every guy who laid eyes on it."

"It's not going to get out. I only sent it to you. I didn't even show it to Rachel or Von."

"Good," he said, running his finger along my chin. "All that ass-kicking would be so exhausting, and I'd rather do this." He pressed up against me and kissed me some more.

By the time we headed home, my skin felt tight and sun-drenched, my hair stank of lake water, and my smile reached so far down inside me I felt like I'd never frown again.

Kaleb had a baseball game to go to, but I didn't even mind. When he wrapped his arms around my waist and kissed me good-bye, I knew that his "boys" didn't really matter. Soon they would go their separate ways and I would be the one sticking around. I would be the one he remembered while he was away. I would be the one whose picture he'd be looking at.

Mom was sitting in the den when I came in, frowning over her computer keyboard. She glanced up when I passed by, and pulled her glasses off.

"Hey, stranger," she said. "You home for the night?"

I rerouted and slipped into the den, sinking into the puffy leather chair beside her desk.

"That's a cute dress. Vonnie's?"

I nodded. "Yeah. But it smells like the lake now. I should wash it before I give it back to her."

Mom smiled. "You have a good time with Kaleb?"

I nodded again, hoping that how much of a good time wasn't registering on my face. She'd have been disappointed to see me rolling around in a bikini with Kaleb, making out in a boat. What would she say about the photo if she knew about it? I couldn't even imagine the lecture I'd get. She would totally freak. I made a mental note to erase the photo from my phone as soon as I got upstairs.

"You look tired. Everything fine?"

"Frog fur," I answered. That was our thing. The way Mom had checked out my mental well-being since as far back as I could remember. It came from something her dad said a lot when she was growing up. If Grampy was having a great day, he'd proclaim he was "fine as frog fur!" If his day wasn't going the way he wanted it to, he'd say, "I'm fine, but my dandy could sure use a tune-up." It had always made Mom giggle. So she passed it on to me. She always asked, "Everything fine?" and I was supposed to answer either "Frog fur" or "Dandy needs a tune-up."

"I'm just tired," I continued. "Didn't get much sleep last night."

"Ah," she said. "Well, neither did I." She put her glasses on and turned back to her computer. "Trying to finalize this budget, and it is not coming together. I don't suppose your father would be willing to trade places with me this week—he can manage the preschool and I'll run the academic world?"

I wrinkled my nose at her. "Doubt it."

Dad and Mom had met in college, both of them majoring in education. They'd graduated, gotten married, and Dad had started teaching fifth grade while Mom got a job directing a preschool. After I was born, she took me to preschool with her every day while Dad worked his way up to principal at his elementary school. He'd been principal for almost as long as I could remember, but then last year, when the superintendent had some sort of public breakdown and it was discovered that the school district needed a whole lot of cleaning up, Dad threw his hat in the ring and got the position. Mom loved her job, even though it didn't pay much, and she loved the little kids she worked with. She always said she was glad it was Dad and not her working for the school district, but she called him Superintendentman and said he was forever "busy saving the world," and when she said those things there was an air of... something behind her voice. Sarcasm? Jealousy, maybe? Dad's job was important, and it seemed like we couldn't go anywhere without someone recognizing him and wanting to talk to him about an issue or a change he'd made.

"Well, then. I suppose I'd better get this budget figured out," she said now. "Eating dinner with us?"

"Sure. I'm going to take another shower first. And maybe a nap."

She wrinkled her forehead and slipped the glasses off again. "You sure you're fine?"

"Frog fur, Mom. Totally."

In fact, I was better than frog fur. After the day I'd had with Kaleb, I was so much better.

I trudged up the stairs to my room, my thighs aching from yesterday's run, my whole body feeling wrung out and dehydrated, but I totally didn't care. I kicked off my flip-flops as I shut the door, then fired up my laptop to check my email.

I had a message from my friend Sarah, whose brother Nate was on Kaleb's baseball team.

It was one sentence.

A sentence I would never forget, no matter how long I lived.

HEY NATE SAID HE SAW A PIC OF YOU NAKED YESTERDAY.

COMMUNITY SERVICE

"Tina wants you to meet with Kaleb," Dad said by way of greeting when I slid into his car after school. I paused, one leg still hanging out the door.

"What?" I hadn't heard my lawyer's name since my court date.

Dad put the car into drive, and I pulled my leg in and shut the door, wrapping the seat belt around myself.

"But I thought the judge wanted us all to stay away from each other," I said. "I'm not supposed to have anything to do with him. Did something happen?"

Dad checked his rearview mirror and pulled into traffic. "Apparently, there is an apology involved. I believe Kaleb's attorney is looking to set it up. I don't know if maybe he's trying to work a plea in his case or something."

My heart thudded in my chest. I hadn't seen Kaleb since the day I slammed his truck door and walked away. I hadn't heard from him since that last, ugly phone call. I'd thought about him lots of times, about how his life had changed, about whether or not he'd decided if everything that had happened was worth it. I'd wondered if he was happy with the way this had all turned out.

Happy.

I remembered when Kaleb and I were happy. Before all the fighting, before all the...everything.

I thought about us curling up against each other on the bus to and from meets. It didn't matter then that he was two years older than I was. Nobody thought twice about it. We were happy. Even after everything that had happened, I still couldn't look at those moments as something bad. Those moments between us were good no matter what. Surely he still saw them as good, too.

"When?" I asked.

"Well, I haven't agreed to it yet," Dad said. "I wanted to make sure you were okay with it. Certainly, I have my own opinions about what he owes you, but if you don't want to see him, I would understand that."

I thought it over. After a day like today, cowering in the library during lunch, walking down the hallways alone while Vonnie and Cheyenne and Annie and all the people I'd once called my friends were joking and laughing and forgetting about me, knowing I would get crap from Kenzie and Angel while doing community service, did I really want to see him?

Would an apology feel like enough? Or would I end up feeling sorry for him? I was so not ready to feel sorry for him.

But I decided that he really did owe me an apology, and even if it was meant to help him reach some plea deal, I wanted to hear it. "Where?"

Dad shrugged, turning into the Central Office parking lot. "I'm not sure. At the courthouse, I suppose. Or maybe at the police station. I'd have to talk to Tina about that." He sounded tired of the subject. The media had continued to hound him over this. He'd been embarrassed, publicly, and I'd even read that some members of the community were going to be at the next board meeting, demanding he step down as superintendent or that the board fire him. He hadn't mentioned any of this at home; I only knew about it from my own research, and I was afraid to bring it up with him.

Mom, too, was tight-lipped about everything that was going on. She put on a smile every evening when I got home. We cooked dinner together, like always. She talked about her kids and about the owner of the preschool, who sometimes drove her nuts. But we never talked about what had happened with the photo. We never talked about what was still happening, with the community service and with Dad. And she never asked me if I was fine anymore. I guessed she already knew the answer to that question.

Or maybe she didn't care. Maybe she figured if I wasn't fine, it was my own fault.

"Would you go with me?" I asked Dad now.

He eased the car into his parking spot and turned it off. "It might be best if Mom went with you to this one, Ash," he said. He didn't sound angry or upset, just weary and afraid. "I'm not sure how close I should be to this now. And I don't know if I could trust myself to be in the same room with him."

I understood where he was coming from. He probably wanted to beat the crap out of Kaleb, and the last thing he needed was the media breaking yet another story involving the Chesterton Public Schools superintendent, this time about him assaulting someone in a courthouse. Especially someone who was trying to apologize. Dad didn't need to look like he was coming unhinged on top of everything else.

We opened our doors, letting the fresh fall air tumble in on us. I took a deep breath, readying myself for another session of community service. "Okay," I said. "Tell her I'll meet with him. It might be good to hear him admit what he did."

And I realized how true that statement really was. How much I wanted, after months of denials and lies, to finally hear Kaleb admit that he'd betrayed me. In some ways, that was all I'd ever wanted from him.

It was too little, too late, but it was something.

The first thing I noticed when I walked into room 104 was that we'd gotten a new kid in Teens Talking. It didn't take long for Kenzie to let everyone know that his name was Cord and that he was there for drugs.

"Total bullshit, though," she whispered to Angel, loudly enough for everyone in the room to hear her. "His principal said he was selling in the parking lot, but nobody ever actually caught him doing it. They searched his locker and everything. Finally, like the third time they searched his car, they found a plastic Baggie and they all starting crying dope on him. I mean, he's been selling since seventh grade, but they didn't have no proof, because he's that good at hiding it."

"Shit, how do you know, anyway?" Darrell said, taking a really long time at Mrs. Mosely's desk with the stapler. Mrs. Mosely had stepped out, leaving all of us alone, including Cord, who was sitting a couple of computers down from me, listening to his iPod. "You don't know nothing."

"Bullshit I don't know nothing," Kenzie shot back. I turned in my chair and could see that the backs of her ears had gone scarlet and she was waving a pair of scissors idly in the air in front of her. Not a threat, but close enough for Darrell to get the hint. "My friend goes to that school and she bought from him all the time." At this point, Kenzie was no longer whispering, and I shot a glance at Cord, who seemed to be oblivious. Which was probably a good thing. I didn't know what they'd do to you if you got in a fight in community service on your first day, but it couldn't be good.

Darrell chuckled. "Your 'friend,'" he said, making quote marks with his fingers. "Right, whatever."

"Yeah, whatever," Kenzie said.

"Why don't you lay off, Darrell?" Angel said, but she said it quietly. Everybody knew Angel and Darrell were friends and had been for a long time. "It ain't about you, anyways."

He glanced at Angel and shook his head. "Kenzie, you're always so full of it. You think you know everything about everything," he said, but he finally snapped the stapler shut on his papers and ambled back to his computer. "Don't know shit," he mumbled as he scooted his chair in.

"That's right, keep talking, Darrell," Kenzie said, then added something under her breath, and she and Angel cracked up.

I went back to my computer, glad nobody had tried to drag me into this. I'd had my share of exchanges with Kenzie—she was always calling me Supermodel and making little comments about getting texts about me. I wished she would finish up that pamphlet or have her baby so she would leave and we could all get some peace.

Mrs. Mosely came back into the room and checked her watch. "Anyone need a restroom break?"

We all got up, like we did every day. Whether you had to use the restroom or not, sometimes the break was needed simply to rest your eyes from the computer or your ears from Kenzie.

We headed down the hallway en masse. Kenzie and Angel made a beeline for the women's restroom, and Darrell ducked into the men's room. Cord stood over by a bulletin board, staring up at it as if it was the most interesting thing he'd ever seen in his life. And Mack went for the candy machine back under the stairs, as he always did.

I wandered near the stairwell, mostly wasting time, but also looking in toward the candy machine. Other than telling

Kenzie and Angel to leave me alone, I had never heard Mack utter a word. Day after day, he sat quietly in his chair, clicking, clicking, clicking his mouse, earbuds in his ears. Mrs. Mosely never asked how his project was going. She never offered to read his work. She never gave him any advice. Not even when she was standing at my computer, her shoulder literally rubbing up against his.

I wondered about Mack. A lot. I wondered what his story was, and how come his was pretty much the only story Kenzie didn't seem to know. Or at least the only story she didn't blab around to everyone else, if she did know.

I watched his shadow as he put coins into the machine and punched some buttons. The denim of his jacket had worn away at one elbow, and his skin, white and pasty, poked through. His pants rode low and were filthy and torn up at the cuffs.

"Want some Hot Tamales?" he asked, and at first I didn't realize he was talking to me.

"Huh?"

He didn't turn around, but repeated, "Want some Hot Tamales?" and then added, "I've got extra quarters if you want something."

"Oh." I took a couple of steps forward, pushing my hair behind my ears. "Okay. Sure."

He plugged a couple of quarters into the machine and pressed buttons. A box of Hot Tamales rattled to the bottom, and he bent to retrieve it. He held it out to me, doing all of this without ever making eye contact.

"Thanks." I took the box and tore it open.

"No problem." He ripped into his box and tossed his chin up, pouring a few candies right into his mouth. I could smell the cinnamon.

I wasn't sure what to say to him. I knew so little about him, it seemed impossible to start a sentence. I was curious, but I didn't want to start prying into his life, asking him a bunch of questions. I liked my anonymity, such as it was, and hated it when Kenzie took it upon herself to talk about my business, so who was I to dig into someone else's personal life?

But I felt like an idiot standing there eating candy and saying nothing, so I asked the least invasive question I could think of.

"You go to Chesterton?"

"Not anymore."

"Oh."

The bathroom doors swished open, and I heard conversation bubbling in the background. In a way, it felt like Mack and I were in a little hiding place in the shadows under the stairs, away from everyone, away from all the drama.

"You used to, though?" I asked.

He nodded, chewing. "Until a few months ago. We had domestic arts together in ninth grade. You were partners with that Vonnie girl."

"She's my best friend. Well...sort of," I corrected. I'd seen Vonnie in the hallway earlier that day. She'd been walking with Will Mabry and he'd had his arm around her. I'd waved to her, wondering when that had happened, when she'd gotten so close to Will, and why she hadn't called me to tell me about it, but she didn't see me wave—or at least I didn't think she saw me—and had walked right on by.

"She's kind of a snot," Mack said. "You should get a better best friend."

I wanted to defend Vonnie, to tell him that she was a great best friend. But at the moment I couldn't do it. I didn't know where Vonnie and I stood. I didn't know if she was mad at me, or if I should be mad at her, and I didn't know if she was still friends with Rachel, which seemed like an impossible barrier between us, even if I could understand that Vonnie felt torn between the two of us after what had happened. It was weird the way Vonnie and I weren't hanging out together anymore. It was like after everything had gone down, she'd moved on without me. She didn't seem mad; she just seemed uninterested.

"We probably should get back before Mosely freaks out on us," I said.

He chuckled. "Mosely's all right," he mumbled, and with that he slid past me and out into the hallway, holding his box of Hot Tamales casually in one hand and completely ignoring Darrell when he tried to get some from him.

I stood in the shadows for a minute longer. What did he mean, I should get a better best friend? And why couldn't I remember this guy if we'd been in the same high school together? Especially if we'd been in the same class together?

But by the time I unrooted my feet and followed him, Mack was already at his computer, earbuds in place.

66

Message 73
Hey girl I don't know if you know this or
whatever but a whole bunch of people are talking
about you. Something about a picture...?
You know what's going on?

I called Kaleb as soon as I read Sarah's email about her
brother seeing the picture I'd sent the night before. My
hands shook around the phone. *What if it got out?* Kaleb
had asked at the lake. Was he asking because he knew it
already had?

"Miss me already?" He was still in his truck, driving.

"Oh my God, Kaleb, how did Nate see my picture?"

Silence, except for the rattle of the truck hitting bumps
on the road. "Huh? What do you mean?"

"Sarah sent me an email saying Nate saw a picture of me naked. Did you show it to him?"

"No. He didn't see it. There's no way. I didn't show anybody."

"Did you tell him about it?"

"Well, yeah, but...I swear I didn't show it to anybody."

My eyes burned. "You told him about it? Did you tell all the guys?"

Another beat of silence. I heard the distant sound of brakes squeaking, the ambient noise of the truck movement fading away. He was stopping. "Don't make a huge deal out of it, Ash."

"It *is* a huge deal to me. I didn't send that picture to you so you could show it around."

"I didn't show it around. I already told you that."

"Then how come Nate says he saw it? God, Kaleb, we had such a fun day, too."

"I don't know why he's saying that. I have no idea, really." He paused, and it sounded like he'd started moving again. "Listen, I've got to go. Don't make a big deal about it. I'll talk to Nate and figure out what's going on. Call you later, okay?"

I closed my eyes and rubbed my temple with my fingers. I didn't believe him. And I'd never had that feeling with Kaleb before. I'd never not trusted him. But somehow I knew he was lying. And I hated that I was now feeling so angry at him after having such a good day together.

"Okay," I said.

"I love you, Ash. I'm the only one who saw that picture."

"Okay," I repeated again, unable to wrap my mouth around the words "I love you," because the only word that my lips wanted to form was "bull."

I hung up and sat on my bed for a while, my eyes glued to Sarah's email.

HEY NATE SAID HE SAW A PIC OF YOU NAKED YESTERDAY.

I stared at those words hard, hoping they would mix and jumble and move around and spell out something different. That they wouldn't be saying what I was afraid of: *Your boyfriend's a liar who betrayed you.*

I heard the front door open and close, the muffled tones of my parents' voices. Dad was home and Mom had probably ambushed him from the den. Soon the smell of dinner would be wafting up to my room and they'd be expecting me to come down.

The scent of the lake water in my hair was suddenly making me nauseous. I groaned and forced myself to get up and take a shower. Only this time I avoided looking in the mirror.

Nate was still at Chesterton. So were two other guys on Kaleb's team. What if they really had seen the picture? I would die every time I saw them in the hallway.

I leaned into the steaming shower spray and willed myself to believe Kaleb. Forced myself to trust that this was no big deal. That Kaleb had bragged to the team about what I'd sent him, and Nate was just being a guy about it. Guys lied about sex all the time. Why wouldn't Nate lie about this? He was probably jealous. He was totally the type to get all envious and then act like he had a part in it somehow.

By the time I got out of the shower, the water was running cold and I'd mostly convinced myself that everything was okay. It would all be fine.

I dressed and headed downstairs, where the smell of chicken curry was so strong it practically singed my nose hairs.

"There she is," my dad said from his spot at the table, his forehead barely peeking out above the top of an open newspaper. It was his evening ritual. Come home, talk Mom down from whatever preschool crisis had her worked up, change into a pair of what he called lounge pants, although they were just a pair of soft, worn khakis, sit down at the kitchen table with the newspaper, and gripe to Mom about the articles while she cooked dinner.

"Hi, Dad." I leaned over the newspaper and kissed his cheek, trying to shrug off the embarrassed feeling that was edging its way in, as if he knew about the photo, too. I knew it wasn't possible, but a few hours ago, I would have said it was impossible that Nate knew about it.

"What did you do today?" Dad asked.

I thought about Kaleb and me making out on his uncle's boat, and my embarrassment deepened. I looked down, afraid I was blushing. "Lake" was all I answered.

"With Vonnie?"

I shook my head. "With Kaleb."

"Ah," Dad said from behind his wall of newspaper. "And when does Loverboy leave for college, again?"

"A few weeks."

"I'll try not to cry," Dad intoned. Dad had never been particularly fond of Kaleb. He didn't have any real reason for disliking him—only that he'd thought Kaleb had "a certain prevaricatory countenance about him" that he didn't quite trust. Mom said it was also because Dad was afraid that Kaleb would take his little girl's innocence away, because that was what boys liked to do. If only Dad knew...

"Stop it, Roy," Mom said from the stove, then tried redirecting. "Make the salad, Ash?"

"Sure," I mumbled, glad to lean into the cold air of the fridge. I lingered there, pretending I was looking for ingredients.

And as I fixed my portion of the dinner, listening to Mom and Dad chat, talking to them about school and cross-country and Kaleb, the sameness of our nightly family ritual made my fear over Nate and the photo worsen rather than get better. What if Nate really had seen it? What if it got around and Mom and Dad found out I had sent it? *What if it got out?*

By the time Vonnie called, asking if I wanted to take a quick spin around the mall, I was a frazzle of nerves, itching to find something to do to take my mind off everything.

"School starts in a week. You can't show up in your old sophomore clothes," Vonnie said as soon as I got into her car, her giant flower ring catching the sun and practically blinding me as she backed out of my driveway. "We're upperclassmen now. It's my duty to make sure you look hot."

I felt dread at the thought of going to school. I hadn't told Vonnie yet about Sarah's email. I didn't want to look hot. Not with Nate and his buddies walking around knowing I'd sent Kaleb that photo. I wished I hadn't ever sent it. If I could have taken it back, I would have.

"I guess," I said, and cranked up the radio all the way to the mall so I wouldn't have to listen to her talk about how she was going to make me sexy.

We wandered around the stores, Vonnie squealing and hopping every time we ran into a "long-lost classmate" we hadn't seen since school let out in May. I stood behind her, chewing on a strand of my hair and thinking about Kaleb. I barely said hello to anyone.

"What's wrong with you?" Vonnie finally asked as she pawed through a rack of cardigans. "You're being really quiet today. And you haven't bought anything."

"Not true," I said, holding up the tiny bag that was looped around my wrist. "Earrings, remember?"

"What, you're going to show up in earrings and your pajamas on the first day? So glam."

I slid some hangers across the rack to look busy. Everything was too dressy or too casual or too bare or too prudish for me. "I'll find something. I'm just not in the mood for shopping."

She peered at me as if I were a stranger, her hand hovering

in midair over a hanger. "I have never known you to not be in the mood for shopping."

I shrugged. "First time for everything, I guess."

"Uh-uh," she said, wagging her finger at me like a schoolteacher, her bangles clanking on her arm. "Something is up. Spill."

I took a deep breath, rubbed my palm over my forehead, then sat down on the nubby carpet.

"I think Nate Chisolm might have seen the picture."

Vonnie looked confused. "What picture?"

"You know. *The picture*. Of me." She still looked confused. "At your party."

Her eyes went wide. She held her hand over her mouth as she sucked in a breath, all of her bangles slamming with a clatter to her elbow. "The nude picture? I totally forgot about that."

"Shhh!" I glanced around. Fortunately, there was nobody nearby. I already wanted to die of embarrassment; the last thing I needed was a crowd. "God, Von, say it louder. I don't think the people in the parking lot heard you."

"Sorry." She sat next to me. "But you do mean the nude picture, right?" she added in a whisper.

I nodded miserably. "Kaleb told the whole team about it, and Nate says he saw it."

"No way. What a jerk."

I rolled my eyes. "It's just...Kaleb says he didn't show it to Nate, but for some reason I feel like he's lying to me.

I mean, why would Nate make it up? Kaleb doesn't want me to make a big deal about it, but…I don't know. I'm still mad."

"Uh, hell yeah, you're mad. I'd be mad at him, too. I can't believe he would do that. Aren't college guys supposed to be more mature?"

"He's not in college yet. And Nate definitely isn't in college." I covered my face with my hands, leaning my elbows on my knees. "What am I going to do?"

Vonnie reached around and rubbed my back softly. "I'm sure it'll be fine, Buttercup," she said. "Nate's probably the one lying and he never saw anything."

"I wish I hadn't sent it," I said into my palms.

"Oh, honey, don't say that. He's going away in a few weeks. You love him. He loves you. Nate's nobody."

"Please don't tell anyone," I said.

"No way," she said, standing up and holding out a hand for me to take. "Not in a million years."

"I hope I don't see Nate for a while. I'll die."

She waved her hand impatiently and made a *pfft!* noise. "Even if it's true and he actually did see it, you probably made his year. Nate's a dork. He won't see another naked girl for, like, his whole life. Unless you take another picture." She pressed her lips together, holding back an evil smile.

"That's not helpful."

She shifted her head to one side. "Seriously, Buttercup. He's most likely already forgotten about it. Everyone has.

Until you brought it up, I had. You're the only one thinking about it right now."

I took her hand and let her pull me up, feeling a little better. She was right. If Nate had seen it, he was probably already over it. In a week he'd be on to something else scandalous. By the end of the year, he wouldn't even remember he'd ever seen it.

I perked up and spent the rest of the evening trying on clothes that fit snug in all the right places, every time wondering what Kaleb would think, how he'd like this outfit or that one. Trying to remember that I loved him and that I'd sent that picture to him because I wanted him to want me. It was okay to want to be desired. Everyone did, right?

We drank milkshakes in the food court with a cluster of friends, including Rachel, who was there with her cousin, and we talked about everything but texting and pictures and Vonnie's party, and by the time Vonnie dropped me off in my driveway, the pang of missing Kaleb was so strong my ribs ached.

Mom and Dad were watching TV in their bedroom, and the rest of the house was dark. I called out that I was home, then headed to the fridge to grab a soda.

My phone rang, and I stood up abruptly, banging the back of my head against the fridge door. I rubbed it, pulling my phone out of my pocket. It was Kaleb.

"Hey," I said.

"I'm sorry, baby. I shouldn't have told them."

I let out a gust of air. "It's okay," I said. "But you're sure you didn't show it to them?"

"Positive. I talked to Nate. He's just being a dick. He won't say any more about it."

"Okay. Good."

"Forgive me?"

I paused. What was there to forgive? After all, I'd told my friends about it, too. Kaleb hadn't been guilty of anything I wasn't also guilty of. "Yeah. Okay. But from now on, what's our business is our business, okay?"

"Yeah, of course. I slipped up once. It won't happen again."

"Okay, good." I climbed the stairs to my room. "Talk tomorrow?"

"Sure. Love you."

"Love you, too."

But even as I hung up, I couldn't help wondering if that was the prevaricatoriness Dad was always talking about that I was hearing in Kaleb's denial.

And I couldn't ignore the little voice in my head that was saying if he slipped up once, who was to say he wouldn't slip up again?

Message 81
Daaaaaamn that's HOT!

We started school on a Tuesday in August. Kaleb drove away the following Thursday afternoon for freshman orientation. The college suggested that the best way for freshmen to battle homesickness during orientation was to avoid contact with home for the entire week so they could concentrate on getting used to living on their own and getting to know the campus.

We stayed out until the very last second of my curfew Wednesday night, kissing and holding each other in his parents' basement as if to make up for time we knew we were going to be missing. I cried when he dropped me off. It felt so final. I didn't know how I'd ever make it through a day, much less a week, a month, a semester without him.

I was a zombie at first, thinking about nothing but Kaleb. About what he was doing and who he was doing it with. So in love and missing him so much it physically hurt. I hadn't seen him as often as I'd wished during the summer. But this was different. At least during baseball season I could stop by if I wanted to, I could see him if I wanted to. With him at college I had no choice but to be away from him.

He didn't call me when his week was up. And he didn't answer when I called, either. I was convinced that something horrible had happened to him, that something horrible had happened to us, so by the time we finally talked, a week and a half after he left, we fought.

I called, and at last he picked up, but he was too busy to talk. In the background I heard plates clinking and girls' laughter.

"I was worried about you. You were supposed to call me days ago," I said.

"I've been really busy. You don't understand. They make you do all kinds of stuff during orientation. You don't have time to talk to anyone. I've barely even talked to my roommate. And I really do have to go."

My eyes felt full and I bit my lip, feeling numb. He was so pulled away, I barely knew his voice. "Okay. Will you call me later?"

"Maybe tomorrow or the next day."

Now my eyes were burning and I knew I was going to cry if this kept up. First his boys, then his orientation, now he was too busy. Why did it seem like there was always something more important to Kaleb than me? But I missed him so much, I wasn't going to say anything. "Okay. I love you."

He paused, and again I heard girls' voices in the background. "Um, I'm not alone in here."

"So what? You can't tell me you love me?"

"Not right now."

"Because there are girls there?"

"No, because there are people here, Ashleigh." His voice was low and breathy in the phone, as though he was cupping a palm over the receiver or talking facing the wall or something. "Don't freak out."

"I'm not freaking out," I said, the tears finally spilling over. I swiped at them. I always cried when I got mad. I hated that about myself. Wished I could be cool and venomous. Icy. Instead, I always turned into a four-year-old, and it was embarrassing. "I don't think it's too much to ask you to tell me you love me. I miss you."

"That's because you don't understand. You're still in high school."

"So now I'm some immature little high schooler? You weren't thinking that last month when you were passing my picture around the table at Pizza Crib."

"I didn't pass that picture around. I've told you that."

"Oh, okay, so Nate just saw it all on his own."

A part of me was surprised that I was bringing up the Nate thing again. Kaleb had sworn he was telling the truth and nobody had seen it, and I'd sworn I believed him, and we'd both promised to let it go, but in my heart I hadn't. I couldn't. Because in my heart, I didn't believe him.

Eventually I let him go back to whatever he had going on that was making him so "busy." We hung up angry, and after that day, he and I could barely talk without our conversation eventually leading to that argument again. It was a nasty loop of me accusing him of lying, of never loving me, and him telling me I was immature and I wouldn't understand what he was going through until I went to college. And one of us would hang up on the other and then three hours later we would text each other, tell each other how sorry we were, that we still loved each other, that we were both stressed out. That I needed to let the picture thing go because I was wrong.

And then one day I saw Nate in the hallway at school. My heart thudded hard in my chest and instantly sweat popped out at my temples. I tried hard to play it off, because I was walking with some girls from cross-country, and I didn't want them to notice that anything was up.

But he looked right at me, gave a little half-wave, then shut his locker door and called out to someone I couldn't see down a connecting hallway and rushed off. And that was it. He looked right through me. There was no "gotcha" moment. No knowing stares. No leers. No comments.

Maybe he really hadn't seen the picture. Maybe Kaleb had been telling the truth this whole time. I felt insanely guilty for all the accusations I'd made.

I called him that night to tell him how sorry I was. To confess to him that I knew he was telling the truth and that I should have trusted him from the beginning because he'd never done anything to make me not trust him and he didn't deserve having me doubt him.

A girl answered his phone.

"Who is this?" I asked, my throat pulling tight and my fingertips tingling.

The perky little voice at the other end said, "This is Holly. Who's this?" And there was this chirpy giggling in the background...a different girl...and some murmuring and a bark of laughter that I would have recognized anywhere. Kaleb.

It took a few seconds for my brain to drown out what was going on in the background and for my mouth to catch up with everything I was thinking, none of which was good at all.

"Is Kaleb there? This is Ashleigh. His *girlfriend*."

I put extra stress on the last word, maybe too much because she made a snorting noise and then I could hear her say, away from the phone, "Kaleb, it's your *girlfriend*," and she put the same stress on the last word as I did. Like she was making fun of me. I felt like a little kid being teased by the big kids in the neighborhood, and anger welled up in me so vigorously my throat felt closed with emotion.

"Hey, Ash," Kaleb said. He had the nerve to sound relaxed, which made me all the madder.

"Having a good time?" I choked out.

"Huh?"

I took a deep breath, but it did nothing to steady my voice. "So who's Holly? Let me guess. She's a study partner."

There was a pause, and I could hear footsteps and the whine of a door closing, like he was getting to someplace private. "Actually, yeah, she is," he said. "You're not going to do this again, are you?"

"Actually, yeah, I am!" I shouted into the phone, no longer in control of my emotions at all. "Every time I call you, you either can't talk or you're giggling with some girls and calling them your study partners, and it's bullshit, Kaleb. Are you sleeping with them?" And there I was again, accusing him of doing something I had no actual proof of. It was like I couldn't stop, I couldn't trust him.

"No," he said, his voice icy and abrupt. "We're part of a study group. There are two guys in there named Mark and Gannon. I'm not sleeping with them, either. Jesus."

"So what was she doing with your phone?"

"It was on the table, and she was the closest one to it. This is stupid. I've got to go. They're waiting for me."

I laughed, a loud, ugly laugh that made me sound pretty much unhinged. And maybe I was. Maybe I finally had lost it. "I'm sure they are. You're totally cheating on me, Kaleb.

I'm not dumb. How would you like it if I cheated on you? How would you feel if you called and some guy answered my phone?"

His already steely voice took on a sharp edge. "I can't even believe you're being that kind of person."

"I'm not!" I shouted, no longer sure what point I was trying to make. I wanted someone to slap their hand over my mouth, to make me stop talking. "I'm trying to show you what it feels like when I call your phone and some girl answers. It feels like crap. You shouldn't think you're the only guy who wants me, Kaleb. Because you're not." It hurt my own heart to say these things, but my mouth had gotten out of my control and there was no bringing it back now.

"Okay, fine. Well, if there's a line at your door, maybe you should go for it. I'm not in high school anymore, and you're acting like a—"

"A high schooler?" I interrupted. "Again? Nice. Maybe that's because I am a high schooler. Which you knew when you started dating me."

"No, actually I was going to say you're acting like a bitch."

The wind was sucked out of me. Kaleb had never called me a bitch before. He'd never called me any name before. I didn't even know what to say. I stood, clutching the phone, my mouth open unbelievingly.

"I've got to go," he said when I didn't respond.

"That's it? You're not even going to apologize?"

"No. Are you?"

I paused. Did I owe him an apology? Should you be sorry for being upset that your boyfriend is hanging out with girls while he's away from you? That one of the girls is answering his phone? That you love him so much the idea of losing him hurts as immediately and fully as if you'd already lost him?

"For what?" I finally said, because I honestly wasn't sure what he wanted an apology for.

"For...just...forget it, Ashleigh. I don't have time for this."

"You don't have time for me, you mean. Because you have Holly to take care of," I spat. I didn't want to end the conversation like this. And if the only way I could keep it going was to keep the fight going, so be it. Plus, I was still wounded. I wanted him to feel bad for what he'd said. I wanted him to feel sorry for me.

"Okay," he said, "bye. I'll talk to you in a few days."

When he finally called, three days later, he was in his car on the way back to Chesterton for a long weekend. He sounded grim. He said he wanted to see me right away. He said we needed to talk.

But he didn't tell me he loved me.

He didn't say he was excited to see me.

Just hung up.

COMMUNITY SERVICE

The day after Mack bought me Hot Tamales, I brought extra change and bought us both SweeTarts. And the day after that I split a packet of Oreos with him because neither of us had enough coins to get a whole pack to ourselves. And pretty soon it was our thing, to head straight for the candy machines during restroom break, me blinking the glow of the computer screen away in the unlit hallway and him yanking up his perpetually falling-down jeans.

Every day we met there, and every day we shared a short conversation. But I was always the one doing the talking.

"Where do you live?" I asked him once.

"In Chesterton."

"Yeah, but where?"

He laughed and stuffed a palmful of M&M'S into his

mouth. "I freaking live here these days." And then I laughed with him, because I totally felt that way sometimes, too, but I soon found myself laughing alone as he took off toward the classroom again. He did that often—just walked away in the middle of a conversation, leaving me feeling awkward and wondering if I'd said something wrong. This time, though, I followed him.

"I live in Lake Heights," I said, tripping after him, the M&M'S in my palm growing warm.

"I know. You live in that green house. The one with the pool."

"No, that's Vonnie's house. Mine's on the smaller side of the neighborhood. You live over there, too, or something?"

"No. Everyone knows about the green house with the pool."

Of course they did. Like I said, Vonnie's parties were legendary.

"What do you listen to?" I asked, pointing to his earbuds, which were casually draped around the back of his neck.

"Music."

I rolled my eyes. "Duh. What kind?"

"Any kind."

"Who's your favorite?"

"Whoever's on at the time."

"Can I listen?"

"Why don't you bring your own music?"

"Because I can't concentrate on that and work at the same time."

"Then I guess you can't listen. I don't want to distract you. Hey, look, a double M&M." He held up two candies fused together, and the subject was closed. Mack had a real knack for closing subjects.

The day before I was supposed to meet with Kaleb, Mrs. Mosely was late and room 104 was locked. Kenzie and Angel sat on the floor, Kenzie's mighty stomach held up by her lap so high it looked like it was eating her head. Angel was painting Kenzie's fingernails, Kenzie's hand splayed out on the carpeted floor in front of them, the scent of finger-nail polish permeating the hallway.

"Damn, girl, close that shit up," Darrell said, dropping his backpack to the floor and leaning against the wall. "You gonna mess up your baby with fumes."

"Shut up about my baby, Darrell," Kenzie said, but he ignored her.

"I got two more to color," Angel said. She glanced up at Darrell. "Then I can do yours." She and Kenzie laughed, and even Darrell seemed to find amusement in her remark.

"Ain't nobody painting my nails," he said. "I'm a real man."

"That ain't what I heard. I heard you got pink toenails up in those shoes," Kenzie said.

Cord made a snickering noise from his place by the bulletin board, and Darrell looked over at him as if he was going to start a fight, but seemed to think better of it. Instead, he said to Angel, "That dude down there is waiting for his turn to get his legs waxed." Cord turned and eyed Darrell.

I pushed away from the wall and headed toward the stairwell, distancing myself before things got ugly. I was surprised to see Mack already there, hands in pockets, assessing his options.

"It's my turn," I said. I pulled a handful of quarters out of my pocket and shook them in my fist. "Big day today. Cinnamon buns."

He took the quarters and fed some of them to the machine. A two-pack of glossy rolls fell to the bottom and he bent to pick them up. I could see that both elbows of his jacket were worn through now. Something about seeing his bare elbows poking out made me feel uncomfortable and spoiled.

"What's the occasion?" he asked, handing me the buns and turning to push more coins into the machine.

I sighed, feeling the heft of the pastry in my hand. "I'm going to see my ex-boyfriend tomorrow."

He raised his eyebrows but didn't respond. Though I figured he already knew, I hadn't shared any of the details of what had happened between Kaleb and me. Kenzie and Angel had said plenty, but I'd never said a word about the photo.

"With my mom and my lawyer. At his lawyer's office. So he can apologize."

He raised his eyebrows again and tore open the plastic over his rolls. "Wow," he said. "Awkward." He pulled a piece of pastry off and popped it into his mouth.

"I know, right? I'm so lucky. He dumped me, called me a bitch, and then ruined my life. I can't wait to see him again," I said sarcastically, but some of the vigor had been leached out of my voice. I didn't like revisiting how it all went down at the end.

A pair of heels clicked down the steps over our heads and we could hear Mrs. Mosely's voice as she apologized for keeping everyone waiting.

"Well, good luck with that," Mack said, and he held up a hunk of cinnamon bun like he was toasting me. I held up my package, too, and bumped it against his hand.

"Thanks."

"For what it's worth," he said, heading down the hallway toward the now open room, "I think he owes you an apology. A lot more than that, actually."

I smiled, even though he couldn't see me. I smiled in the shadows underneath the stairs and the soft glow of the backlighting from the candy machine, because I believed him. And I agreed with him. Kaleb owed me more than an apology. A lot more.

Eventually I made my way to the classroom, where Mrs. Mosely was giving a lecture about behavior in the hallways even when she was tardy and how it was inappropriate to deface public property with fingernail polish or anything else, and I knew I'd missed something that had happened with Kenzie and Angel and Darrell, but I didn't really care. The three of them didn't want me in their little triangle any more than I wanted to be in it.

I laid my community service paper, which was getting pretty filled up with signatures, on Mrs. Mosely's desk and headed for my computer. Mack was already clicking away on his. I sat down, opened my cinnamon buns, and took a small bite before pulling up my browser.

After a few minutes, I felt a bump on my shoulder. I looked over to see Mack's hand, holding out an earbud toward me. The other earbud was in his right ear, and I could hear the buzzing of electric guitars coming out of this one. I took it and put it in my ear.

And for the first time in what felt like forever, I smiled.

SEPTEMBER

Message 94
OMG, that is gross!

Message 96
Srsly? Uncool. For real.

I dressed in tight capris and a tank top. Showered, did my hair, put on makeup, tried to look extra good for him. Sat on my front porch and waited, craning my neck to look down the street every time I heard a car engine.

When he finally showed up, I smiled bright and kissed him hard and let tufts of his hair, which had gotten longer while he'd been away, slide between my fingers.

"God, it's so good to see you," I said, wrapping myself around him. He smelled amazing, and memories of all the things we'd done together flooded in on me and made me melt a little on the inside. Suddenly our fights didn't matter to me anymore. It seemed impossible that this guy would ever have hurt me.

I remembered the night he'd asked me to prom last year. Out of the blue, he'd shown up at my house carrying a big white box. He was already tan from baseball practice and he'd bought a new cologne—the one he was wearing tonight—and he looked nervous and excited. He was wearing the silver chain I'd given him for Christmas, and his hair curled out from under his baseball cap, a little tuft poking through the hole in the back. I'd opened the door and he'd handed me the box without saying a word. Inside were a dozen cupcakes, almost too beautiful to eat, and on the ones in the center, the words ASHLEIGH WILL YOU GO TO PROM WITH ME? were piped on with pink icing. We'd sat on my front porch and devoured as many of them as our stomachs could handle, feeding each other and joking about the insane number of pictures our moms were probably going to take. That night was magical, and prom night was even more magical than that.

I wanted to get some of that magic back. "I missed you," I said, squeezing hard.

He didn't answer. And his arms felt limp around me. But when I pulled away, he offered a half-smile. He looked tired, like he hadn't had much sleep the night before.

"Where to?" I asked, climbing into the passenger side of

his truck. Even though things had been tough between us lately, I had been sure that when we saw each other face-to-face everything would be great.

He got behind the wheel and we closed the doors. But he didn't turn the key, and instead sat there looking red in the face.

I touched his arm, trying to ignore the pangs of alarm beating through my fingertips. "What's up?" I asked.

Finally, he turned toward me, leaving his keys dangling in the ignition, the truck turned off.

"You look really pretty tonight." He picked up a handful of my hair and let it fall back against my shoulder.

I smiled. "Thank you. All for you." I scooted toward him and leaned in to kiss him, but he turned away from me.

"Listen, Ash." He cleared his throat, then paused, and my smile crumpled in on itself. I already knew what this was before he ever said a word.

"You're breaking up with me," I said, my voice brittle and bitter. A statement, not a question.

He nodded, closing his eyes miserably.

"Because of her, right?" He looked confused. "Holly?" I prodded, and he rolled his eyes and shook his head like he'd known I was going to go there.

"In a way, I guess you could say that."

"I knew it!" I said. "I knew you were sleeping with her."

"I wasn't! And I'm not. But it's...this. It's the way you're always accusing me of stuff. Always starting fights. I can't take it anymore. I can't keep making you feel miserable and letting you make me feel guilty when I didn't even do anything wrong."

I crossed my arms and cocked my jaw and stared straight ahead, catching my own reflection in the window. Strangely, there were no tears this time. I was so angry I felt shaky, but my eyes were dry.

"Excuse me for loving you," I said sarcastically. "I'm so sorry I cared that you were falling in love with someone else."

"See?" he said, his own voice taking on that clipped, pissed sound it'd had so often lately. "That's what I'm talking about. You assumed I was falling in love with someone else, so you started accusing me of it. You are constantly accusing me of things I didn't do."

"But I always say I'm sorry. That's what couples do when they fight. They apologize and work it out. They don't just give up when they go through a hard time."

He paused, licked his lips, and then said, "But I don't want to work it out anymore. I don't want to be with someone who's always having to say she's sorry. And I want to give up."

I sat back and let it sink in. Kaleb really was breaking up with me, and there was nothing I could do about it. I knew I would be heartbroken over losing him, but at the moment I was so furious that he'd come all this way, and had led me to believe that he wanted to see me, and I was so foolish and desperate to keep him that I'd jumped at the chance to believe that this little visit of his was going to be all about repairing our relationship. And why? Why had I been so desperate to keep him? So I could continue to be left out while he played baseball and hung out with his study groups at college?

"Fine," I spat. "I deserve better than this, anyway. I deserve someone who appreciates me without making me beg for attention. You know, I never complained when you chose baseball over me. I always sat behind the dugout in my stupid little lawn chair, watching you, instead of going out and doing something fun with my friends. I didn't say anything when you blew off Vonnie's party. I even sent you that picture to show you how much I loved you and to make our relationship more real. What a crock."

He blinked, like he was confused, and then it seemed to dawn on him what I was talking about. "I didn't ask you to send that picture."

"And I didn't ask you to share it with Nate!"

He threw his head back and made a moaning, growling noise. "That again? God, it's like you can never drop anything, Ashleigh. I did nothing wrong. You're imagining it all."

"You admitted you told Nate about it. I'm not imagining that. And that's what started our problems."

He shook his head again. "Ridiculous. Actually, you're what started our problems. I could never be with you long-term. You're psycho."

"Screw you, Kaleb," I said, and grabbed the door handle. "Are we done?"

He nodded. "More than."

"Good. It was so nice knowing you," I said, sarcasm dripping off my tongue. I could feel the tears coming at last, and I wanted to get out of the truck before he had the satisfaction of seeing me cry. "Thank God I never slept with you. You're probably a walking STD."

"Whatever. Says the girl who takes pictures of herself naked at parties."

I glared at him, wishing like crazy I'd never listened to Rachel at that party. Had never sent him anything. The way he said it, like taking nude photos of myself was something I did all the time, made me feel more than embarrassed. It made me feel ashamed. "You better delete that picture from your phone," I said.

He made a disgusted face. "Believe me, I did that a long time ago."

I slammed the truck door and ran inside, keeping the tears at bay until I was safely upstairs in my bedroom. I fell facedown onto my bed and cried until I was spent.

Then I called Vonnie.

"What's up, Buttercup?" she singsonged into the phone. I could hear the squeak of shoes on a gym floor in the background. "Sorry, just got done with volleyball practice. Waiting for Annie to get out of JV practice. Can you believe she didn't make varsity again? She's thinking of quitting. I don't blame her. I mean, seriously, if you've been playing since you were nine and your coach won't even put you on varsity junior year, that's pretty messed up."

"Yeah," I said with no conviction in my voice. "I guess."

"Uh-oh. You sound upset. Should I start a petition?" She laughed. "Just kidding. What's up with you?"

I sniffled and pulled a thread on my bedspread, watching the fabric bunch and snag. "Kaleb and I broke up."

She gasped. "What? When?"

"Just now. He's in town."

The coach's whistle trilled and I had to pull the phone away from my ear. When I put it back, Vonnie was in mid-sentence. "—happened? What did he say? Was it about that other chick he's been hanging out with?"

The thread I was pulling snapped, so I dug up another and yanked harder. The fabric scrunched in on itself. "No. I mean...kind of. He said I was psycho for always accusing him of cheating on me."

"How could he blame you? I mean, he's, like, always with her, isn't he? This is a diversion tactic. He's totally sleeping with her and he doesn't like that you busted him on it."

"I don't know, Von. He swears he wasn't. Isn't. Why would he lie if he was going to break up with me anyway? I mean, why not just admit it?"

"Um, because he's a guy? That's my guess. Lying is all they know how to do."

"Yeah, I guess," I said, though I wasn't sure if I believed it. Ever since Russell had broken Vonnie's heart, she'd been convinced that all guys were as horrible as he was. The second thread snapped and I rolled it into a ball between my thumb and forefinger. "It doesn't matter. It's definitely over between us."

"I'm sorry, Buttercup. But really, you're better off without him. He was always hanging out with those baseball wannabes and you were always alone. And then he moves away and he gets all freaked out because you miss him?" She made a grunting noise into the phone. "He's not worth the trouble. Now you can find a real guy."

I felt tears threatening to start anew, mainly because I didn't agree with her. Kaleb had been worth it. I'd dated him the longest I'd ever dated anyone. We'd had a lot of good times, before summer break. As mad as I was at him now, it was impossible to forget how happy I'd been with him then.

There were more whistles and the sound of shoes pounding on wood floor. "Oh, hey, Annie's done. Gotta go. I'll call you later, okay?"

"Okay," I said, curling into a ball on my side, pressing the phone between my ear and the bed so I wouldn't have to hold it.

"Don't worry. You'll be glad he's gone in no time. You say he's in town for a couple days?"

"Yeah. For the weekend."

"At his parents' house?"

"I would assume so."

"Okay. Good." And then she hung up.

And I drifted off to a dark, dreamless sleep. It wasn't until I woke up again an hour later that it occurred to me what she'd said. What had she meant, *good*?

COMMUNITY SERVICE

Kaleb's lawyer's office was one of those hoity-toity stuffy places where all the furniture was burgundy leather and there was soft lighting through cream lampshades, and classical music was being piped in from somewhere, but you could only hear it if you were very, very still. It was the kind of place where you felt like you had to whisper, as if loud voices weren't allowed.

I had been shaking when I pushed open the door, unsure of what to expect. I'd seen Kaleb's pickup truck in the parking lot, and something about knowing he was right here in the same building I was about to be in made me extraordinarily nervous. I was going to see him for the first time since we broke up, and I didn't know what that would mean. Would I miss him? Get that old butterfly feeling in my stomach again? Cry? God, please tell me I wouldn't cry.

Tina walked up to the front desk and waited for the receptionist—a svelte lady with perfectly straight brown hair and glossy lips—to slide open the glass that separated her from the waiting room.

The last time I'd spent any time with Tina was during my court date. I'd been so scared, I'd just stared at the stains in the industrial carpeting of the courtroom, which was nothing like any courtroom I'd ever seen on TV. It was more like the meeting room in Central Office. A long conference table surrounded by ten or so swiveling office chairs. The judge wore jeans under his robe and spoke in a tired, lazy drawl.

The other seats had been occupied by the attorneys. An attorney from the DA's office, who wore a beige suit and carried an expensive-looking briefcase, sat next to a much younger woman in an overwhelming navy wool suit. She subtly nodded every time he spoke and handed him documents at precisely the right moment.

Tina, who my parents had hired right after our first meeting with the police, sat next to me. She looked unkempt compared to the other lawyers, hobbling in on a pair of low heels, a skinny woman with incredibly frizzy hair and a great, scowling mouth.

I had sat quivering in my chair as the attorneys and the judge went through the timeline of events that had led me there—me sending the photo while drunk at a party, the breakup, and the events that unfolded after the breakup. Tina pointed out that I was, technically, a victim of what had happened, not a perpetrator.

"We're not out to add insult to injury, Your Honor," the beige-suited attorney had responded. "We're sympathetic to what has happened to Miss Maynard, and we agree that she is also a victim. But we need to set a precedent. Sending nude photos of minors is distribution of child pornography, and we feel the need to make a statement to teens if we're going to help stop this behavior."

The judge had nodded, said a few technical things to Tina and the others, and then looked at me.

"Miss Maynard, it seems you've learned a hard lesson here."

I nodded. "Yes, sir."

He paused, thought, then issued the order for community service.

And it was over.

Mom had held my hand as we left the courtroom. Dad had led us through the lobby. I followed behind, hearing my parents and Tina say words like "lucky" and "good judge" and "went easy," and I saw my dad shake Tina's hand and thank her, and I felt like I was supposed to be thanking her, too, and be grateful for what had happened in there, but I couldn't. I'd watched her walk away, her wiry hair bobbing through the crowd, and hoped that I would never have a reason to see her again.

But here I was, in yet another lawyer's office, staring at the back of her frizzy head as she stood expectantly before the receptionist's window.

"Here to see Mr. Frank?" the receptionist whispered when she opened the glass.

Tina nodded. "Yes. Ashleigh Maynard?" She said my name like it was a question, like she wasn't sure if I was supposed to be here or not. Honestly, I felt like I wasn't. Had she said, "You know, we've made a mistake. We're not here to see Mr. Frank," I would have gladly gotten up and raced back outside. Forget Kaleb's apology—I didn't need it after all.

A few minutes later, a door opened and a man in a tidy suit stepped into the waiting room. He nodded to Tina and then held out his hand to Mom. "Mrs. Maynard? I'm Byron Frank, Kaleb's attorney."

Mom stood and shook his hand, though she looked like she didn't really want to. She pushed her purse strap farther up on her shoulder and took a few confident steps toward the door. "You can call me Dana. And this is Ashleigh."

Mr. Frank nodded at me and then looked away, as if I didn't exist. It occurred to me that maybe he'd seen the photo, and the thought made me feel every bit as uncomfortable as he seemed to be. It was one thing to think about the boys at school having seen me naked; it was another thing altogether to think about grown men who might have seen it. I pushed the thought away, too nervous to worry about that for now. I didn't need any more to worry about.

Mr. Frank turned so his back was propping the door open and held one arm out to invite us inside.

"Kaleb's waiting for us in the conference room. Would you like something to drink?"

Mom and I shook our heads and followed Tina through the door. The interior of the office was as fancy as the lobby. There was even a chandelier hanging in the hallway, throwing light around in geometric shapes on the walls. No wonder the receptionist whispered. If I'd worked in a place so fancy, so stuffy, I'd have felt like whispering, too. Or maybe I'd have the uncontrollable urge to make a really loud noise, do a cartwheel, whoop and holler, if for no other reason than to make sure I was alive.

Tina and Mr. Frank strode forward, letting the door close and leading us down the hallway. They talked to each other quietly, and we couldn't hear what they were saying. Finally, Mr. Frank glanced over his shoulder at Mom and me. "Thank you for coming," he said. "This is important for Kaleb."

"Why?" I asked, and I realized it came out kind of snotty and disbelieving, but I really was curious. "I mean, what made him decide to do this?" I said a little more softly.

Mr. Frank slowed down. "He feels a lot of remorse over what happened," he said. "He wants you, and the court, to understand that."

"Oh," I said, even though I wasn't so sure I believed that Kaleb felt all that much remorse. He hadn't seemed so remorseful the last time we'd talked. I did, however, believe that he wanted the court to understand how remorseful he was. I would, too, if I were looking at the kind of trouble Kaleb was in.

No matter what Mr. Frank said, I knew why Kaleb was giving me this apology. He wasn't giving it because he really felt sorry. He was giving it because someone had told him to. Because he was hoping it would help him out. He hadn't had his court date yet—the fact that he was an adult made his situation a whole lot stickier than mine—and according to my dad, it wasn't likely that he was going to get off with community service, as I had. Maybe apologizing to me and my family would help the judge see him favorably. That wasn't really an apology, was it? He wasn't really sorry. He was only sorry for the kind of trouble he was in now.

We reached a room that was all windows, covered with closed Venetian blinds. Mr. Frank paused, resting his hand on the doorknob. "I'm hoping you'll have an open mind with my client," he said, and I wasn't sure if he was addressing me or Mom or Tina or all of us.

"Of course," Tina said, her hair shivering every time her mouth opened. "I hope he'll have an open mind, too."

Mr. Frank gave a half-nod, then opened the door and gestured for us to go in.

Tina turned to me. "You ready?" she asked, and attempted a sympathetic smile, though it looked so uncomfortable on her, I guessed she wasn't used to making gentle overtures. I nodded, and Mom reached over and squeezed my hand.

Kaleb sat at the far end of the long table, a soda and a piece of paper in front of him. I paused, waiting for something to happen. For my heartbeat to speed up or my throat to constrict or my belly to wobble or rage to well up in me or...anything.

But he appeared so small. And skinny, very skinny. He had definitely lost weight since I'd last seen him. And he had dark circles under his eyes. He barely resembled the Kaleb I'd once kissed. He looked a lot older, and like he was sick. All I could feel was shock that this was my ex-boyfriend.

He watched us as we walked in, but he made no move. His hands remained in his lap, his paper and soda remained untouched. He showed no emotion on his face. And I couldn't take my eyes off of him. Even though I knew there were three other people in the room, it was as if my gaze had simply zoned in on him and we were the only two there.

Mr. Frank came in and shut the door behind him, moving briskly to a chair at Kaleb's side and folding his hands on the table.

"You sure I can't get you anything?" Mr. Frank asked Mom and me, and again we mumbled "no." "Okay, well, we don't want to drag this out," he said. "Mr. Coats feels that he should apologize to you for his part in what happened, and he has prepared a statement to that effect. Kaleb?"

His part in what happened, I thought sourly. *His part was every part of what happened. Without his part, nothing would have happened.*

Kaleb gazed at his attorney and then slowly, slowly

picked up his paper. It wiggled in the air and I knew his hands were shaking. I found a tiny bit of joy in that. He cleared his throat.

"Ashleigh and Mr. and Mrs. Maynard," he said. He paused, made eye contact, looked back down. "I mean, I guess just...uh, Mrs. Maynard. The past few months have not been easy for me, as I am sure they have not been for you, either. I have had a lot of time to think about what I did, and it has come to my attention that I owe you all an apology. Mrs. Maynard, I am sorry that I have brought embarrassment to your family. I realize that my actions have caused you hardship in your professional life as well as your personal life, and I am very sorry." He paused and made eye contact again, and I was surprised to see Mom nod at him, not unkindly.

"Thank you," she said quietly. She didn't add that his apology was accepted, and I knew that with Mom that was purposeful—that his apology wasn't accepted, because a few rehearsed sentences weren't good enough. Not for what he'd done to our family. Not for what he'd done to my dad's job.

Kaleb shifted his eyes to me, and for the first time I did feel something. Something—I don't know—nostalgic. A longing for what once was. I realized how much I had really grown to hate him, and how much I wished I hadn't had to. But I knew I'd never have him back. I'd never have us back, not the way we used to be. It wouldn't be possible after everything that had happened. I wanted to have that innocence back—the kind of innocence where I would never believe that a boy I loved would hurt me.

He cleared his throat again, adjusted the paper in his hands. "Ashleigh, I know I've caused you a lot of pain. I have violated your trust and your sense of privacy, and I am sorry. I am also sorry for all of the things that you've had to go through. I'm sorry that people have been saying things about you and that you have to do community service, because you never meant to hurt me with that photo, but I meant to hurt you with it, and that was wrong."

I didn't say anything. When he finally looked up, I sat there woodenly, even though I could feel Mom's and Mr. Frank's heads turn toward me. Hearing Kaleb speak made me feel numb and heavy, and I wasn't big enough to thank him for the apology, or worse, to tell him it was okay.

"I hope you can forgive me," he said with finality, and then he set the paper down on the table and placed his hands back in his lap.

We all sat there in uncomfortable silence for a few long minutes. I knew everyone was expecting me to say something, but I couldn't do it. *That was it?* I wanted to shout. *You said nothing! You apologized for nothing! A bunch of vague words that your attorney probably wrote for you!*

I wanted out. I wanted to leave. To get away from this sunken boy and stop hearing him talk about it. I wanted to be done with the whole mess. To have things go back to normal. To go back to a place where I could walk down a hall without people whispering about me. To go back to when my parents trusted me and we were close. To go back to knowing exactly who my friends were, and who would betray me. I needed that more than I needed apologies. How could I ever have thought that Kaleb's apology would be enough? Even if it had been a sincere one?

"Okay," Tina finally said. "Thank you."

She and Mr. Frank talked about Kaleb's upcoming court date, but I didn't hear what they were saying. The emotions and thoughts and feelings of injustice that had been building up inside me since this whole thing began crashed together. I felt like I was being swept away, moved by them, swayed by them. Every time I looked down, there were my hands, resting comfortably on the table in front of me. There were my legs, stretched across the burgundy leather of the conference room chair. There was my mom, looking subtly angry and disappointed and sad. How could we all look so calm and in control?

"We appreciate you coming," Mr. Frank said, pushing his chair away from the table and starting to stand up, checking his watch as if this meeting was just another line in his schedule book. He probably had to move on to bigger and better clients, bigger and better cases. This was our lives, but it was another to-do for him. And all the while my thoughts and emotions consumed me, needed to be let out.

"I didn't do anything to hurt you," I blurted out, and Mr. Frank lowered himself back into his seat. He looked at

Kaleb. "After we broke up, I left you alone. I let you go. Why did you do it, Kaleb?"

Kaleb looked down into his lap, shaking his head slowly. "I don't know." He looked up at me, and I could see pain in his eyes. "But just so you know, I didn't think it would all get so out of hand. I had no idea it would turn into all this. I thought it would just stay with a few people."

"So your goal was only to completely humiliate me a little bit? Gosh, thanks, I feel so much better now."

"No, my goal was to...I don't know." He rubbed his hands over his hair. "I was pissed off, and it wasn't smart or right. It just happened. And I'm sorry that I did it."

"Sorry that you did it or sorry that you got in trouble for it?" Because I was willing to bet he wouldn't have been sorry at all if he'd never gotten caught. "What exactly are you sorry about, Kaleb?"

"Ms. Culver," Mr. Frank said to Tina, "our intention was not to give your client a platform to attack Mr. Coats. We're here for an apology."

Tina's giant mouth flopped open. "N-no, of course not," she stammered. "But, understandably, my client has some thoughts she wants to express—"

"I think the least he can do is answer some questions for my daughter, don't you?" Mom said, interrupting Tina. She placed her hand on the back of my chair.

Mr. Frank held out his hand to Mom but spoke to Tina. "Now, I understand that Miss Maynard was hurt by this unfortunate mistake. But you need to understand that Mr. Coats has been hurt by it as well. Maybe more than she has."

"And you need to understand that this was no mistake," Mom said, her voice ratcheting up a notch. "You heard him say he deliberately did what he did. That doesn't sound like any sort of accident to me."

Mr. Frank's hand hovered over the table, and I could almost see him kick himself into lawyer mode. His face got very serious and his body language changed. He sat forward, his palm spread toward Mom as if he were trying to physically hold her down. Tina must have sensed something, too. She stood up and gathered her things as if to usher me out quickly. "It was a mistake in judgment. He has admitted as much. But, again, we're not here for—"

"It's okay," Kaleb interrupted. He took a deep, shuddering breath. "I'll answer her." He turned to me. "What I'm sorry about is that I didn't break up with you the day before I turned eighteen," he said. "And I don't mean that in a mean way or anything. It's just that if I'd broken up with you then, I wouldn't be in..." He trailed off, shook his head, paused. I could see moisture glistening under his eyes. I almost felt dizzy with surprise; here I'd been worried that I might cry in front of Kaleb, and he was the one crying in front of me instead. "I wouldn't be in this mess," he finally said, and I could see his Adam's apple moving up and down as he swallowed away his tears. "They're calling that picture child pornography. If I get charged, I could have to register as a sex offender. I want to be a teacher, Ashleigh, and sex offenders don't get to be teachers. I'll have to move out of my parents' house, because they live down the street from my old elementary school. People will naturally assume that I'm some sick pervert, and you know that's not true. We never even had sex. I never even asked you to. I never asked you to send that picture in the first place. So I'm sorry that I didn't break up with you sooner, and if I could take back everything that's happened, trust me, I would."

Mr. Frank had lowered his hand into his lap and had taken up a cocky, crossed-legged pose. He checked his watch again. "If we're satisfied...?"

"Ashleigh?" Tina said. "Do you have anything else you'd like to say?"

I shook my head. What was there left to say? We were both screwed, and all because of some dumb, childish payback game.

Mom stood, shouldered her purse. "Well, I'm sorry for all you've gone through, Kaleb," she said. "But you chose to do what you did. My husband, on the other hand, is probably going to lose his job over something he had nothing to do with. You chose that for him."

"Dana..." Tina said in a soft warning voice.

Mr. Frank stood, too, and hitched the waistband of his pants. "I'm going to have to stop you there, Mrs. Maynard, because that's not what we're here for today and Mr. Coats and I have another appointment, so we'll need to adjourn this meeting." So much for the congenial host Mr. Frank had been when we'd arrived. Our time was up and we needed to leave—he'd made that crystal clear.

"Yes, I think we're done here," Mom said. "We can find our way out." She headed for the door. I followed behind, glancing back at Kaleb one last time. He was staring down at the rumpled paper on the table, rubbing his gaunt cheeks with his hand. He looked up and our eyes met before I very quickly looked away, concentrating on the back of Tina's head as we walked out.

I'd finally told Kaleb exactly how I felt. Problem was, I didn't feel any better at all than I had when I walked into the room. I might even have felt worse.

COMMUNITY SERVICE

Dad had a meeting, so he picked me up right after school the next day to drop me off at community service. I was early, but I didn't really mind all that much. When we pulled up, Mack was sitting on a concrete bench out in front of the double doors, the collar of his jean jacket pulled up over his ears against the chilly fall wind.

I joined him, dropping my backpack between my feet.

"Hey," I said.

Mack nodded. I could hear music blasting through his earbuds, but somehow he could still hear me. The wind gusted and I pulled my jacket tighter around me. I liked the cold against my cheeks. It woke me up. In some ways it was the most awake I'd felt all day.

"You been here long? Your cheeks are red," I said.

He shrugged. "A while," he said.

"Can I listen?" I held out my palm and after a hesitation, Mack pulled out an earbud and placed it in my hand. I put it in, tapping my foot along with the music, which was some dubstep song I'd never heard before. We sat together through the whole song, neither of us needing to say anything, neither of us acknowledging the cold.

The song ended.

"How'd it go yesterday?" Mack asked, thumbing the volume down. He didn't look at me, but instead focused his eyes off across the bus yard, which was next door to the Central Office building. Buses were pulling out of the parking lot, their engines roaring.

"Terrible."

He chewed his bottom lip, and for a long moment I thought that was going to be the end of it, but he simply watched another bus pull away, then said, "So I take it his apology didn't make you feel any better?"

"That's the thing," I said. "He didn't apologize. Not really. He said he was sorry for how things turned out, and he talked about how bad it's been for him, but he never really said anything specific, you know?" And I realized that was probably what bothered me about my meeting with Kaleb the most. You could have plugged that apology into pretty much any situation and it would have worked. It was as good as saying nothing at all.

"You wanted him to apologize for something specific?"

Finally, Mack turned to me. The gray sky reflected in his eyes and made them darker.

I pulled the earbud out of my ear and held it in my lap, staring down at it. "No. I wanted him to apologize for everything specific." I shook my head. "I know that doesn't make sense. I just..." I watched the buses some more, trying to come up with the right words. "I just wanted him to say it. To say what he'd done. It was like he admitted nothing."

Mack turned his gaze back to the bus yard, where two men were talking animatedly beside a bus that had its hood propped open. He nodded, as if he was mulling over what I'd said.

"Hearing him say it wouldn't make it go away, though," he said after a moment.

"No, I suppose it wouldn't," I agreed.

He turned up the volume again, and I put the earbud back into my ear, and we sat and listened to music until Mrs. Mosely walked past us on the sidewalk, hugging a book in her arms, her purse slung sideways across her chest.

"You better get inside before you freeze to death, you two," she said.

We watched her push through the front doors, and we sat there for a few minutes longer. And then, without speaking, I handed the earbud back to Mack, and we both got up and walked in behind her.

SEPTEMBER

I pushed a piece of pancake around on my plate, making a design with the butter and syrup streaks it left behind.

My father's voice, which had been droning on and on for what seemed like forever, drifted in and out of my consciousness. "...man's a pompous ass...thinks the whole world owes...ought to tell him..."

My mom made conversational noises to show she was listening. Little "uh-huhs" and "mmms" and soft gasps while she nibbled on bites of oatmeal.

Dad had been going on about this for days now.

Something about the board president, who Dad had never gotten along with, ever. The guy had taken to publicly calling out my dad for doing a poor job with some recent budget cuts. Dad had been moping around the house, snarling at the TV, barking things into the telephone, drinking glasses of wine at record speed, and griping at every meal, especially breakfast, as he faced another day of dealing with the fallout of the board president's words at work.

"...going to have to talk to the newspaper yourself, I suppose..." Mom was saying. I sipped my orange juice and eyed the clock, trying to rally myself into wanting to go to school. After breaking up with Kaleb, I was so depressed I barely wanted to move, much less go listen to teachers for seven hours. But thinking about Kaleb only made my tears begin anew, and I was so tired of crying. I did not want to be one of those girls—the ones who shuffle through school sniveling into a tissue and tearfully announcing their latest breakup to anyone who's unlucky enough to get in their path or dumb enough to ask what's wrong.

"I have to get to school," I finally said, standing and taking my plate to the sink.

Both of my parents looked up, Dad's rant temporarily forgotten. "You didn't eat anything," Mom said.

"I'm not very hungry today. Plus, we're eating doughnuts in math," I lied. "For passing some test."

"Oh, congratulations, honey!" Mom said, but Dad bellowed over her, pointing his fork in my direction, "See?

They blame me for the budget problems, but as long as the teachers are cramming food down the throats of every kid who gets an A on a test..."

I edged for the door, picking up my backpack and sliding into my flip-flops.

Mom tilted her head and sized me up, ignoring Dad. "You fine?" she said. She looked suspicious.

I willed a smile. Tried to look casual. "Frog fur, Mom, I promise. I just ate a lot last night, I think."

"Well, you call me if you feel sick or anything, okay?"

"Of course." Vonnie's car horn honked two short beeps and I jumped. "Von's here." I took two steps back into the kitchen and kissed Mom on the cheek. "Have a good day at school," I said.

She smiled. "Hey, that's my line." Another of our goofy inside jokes.

I raced outside and immediately heard music coming from Vonnie's car. Cheyenne and Annie were in the backseat, and they were all talking over each other and the song, which was turned up so loud the thumping bass was bouncing off the sides of my neighbors' houses. I saw Mrs. Donnelly sitting in a rocker on her front porch, her pink robe cinched tight around her middle, a coffee mug pressed against her lap. I grinned at her and waved; she nodded grimly.

When I opened the car door, noise spilled out like I'd opened the door into a rave. Vonnie was laughing so hard she was dabbing at the corners of her eyes with her fingertips, trying to keep mascara from running down her face.

I plunked into the passenger's seat and held my backpack in my lap. Cheyenne and Annie were singing at the tops of their lungs, their Starbucks cups sweating in their hands. It was hot outside, the kind of day that made you wish it was still summer break and that they waited to start school until after the crappy gray weather rolled in for the season, rather than in August.

"Yo, Buttercup!" Vonnie shouted. "Sorry, we hit the fraps without you. We're draggin' ass big-time this morning." She eyed the backseat through the rearview mirror, and they all cracked up.

"No problem," I said, not getting what was so funny. I looked back and forth between them. "What?" I asked.

"Nothing," Vonnie said, too innocently. "I swear."

We pulled out of the driveway and headed toward the highway.

"Dude, I seriously think I pulled something in my knee last night," Annie said, leaning forward and turning down the music. "I fell right into that ditch. I had grass stains on my skin, for real. Not on my clothes, but on my *skin*."

"I still have shoe polish on my right hand," Cheyenne said. "You were so lucky that neighbor pulled right into his garage, Annie. He'd have seen you for sure."

"I know. That's why I ran into the ditch. I was freaking out."

"What?" I asked again. "What did you guys do last night?" Again, they all met eyes in the rearview mirror, but nobody said anything. After a beat, they broke into a new round of laughter. "No, really," I said. "What are you talking about?" I was starting to get irritated, even though their stupid smiles were making me smile, too.

"Vigilante justice," Vonnie said.

"More like knee rearrangement," Annie said.

I still didn't get it. "Whatever. Don't tell me."

Finally, Vonnie turned off the radio and glanced at me as she navigated the morning highway traffic. The turnoff to the school was backed up, as usual. "Vigilante justice," Vonnie repeated. "We righted a wrong."

"Totally," Cheyenne said around her straw, then belched. Annie called her gross and threw a wadded-up napkin at her.

"Spill it," I said, a smile creeping in. Whatever it was, it must have been crazy, from the sound of things. I felt a little pang of jealousy that they hadn't asked me to do it with them.

My phone buzzed. A text. I looked at it and my breath caught. It was from Kaleb. Part of me was angry that he was already texting me after saying he never wanted to talk to me again, and part of me hoped he was apologizing and asking me back. I opened the text, barely breathing.

All it said was: WTF?!

I was pretty sure he hadn't meant to text me, because I had no idea what he was talking about. Probably he'd meant to send it to Holly or whichever college girl he'd broken up with me for.

I texted back: ???

Vonnie inched forward behind a van, which we were pretty sure belonged to one of the sophomores' mommies.

Car stratification was very important in our school. You could always tell who was who by what they drove. Minivan or Volvo? A sophomore driving his parents' car. Old-fart car with bumper stickers that said stuff like MY OTHER CAR IS A TRUCK, half ripped off? A junior with her first wheels of her own. Brand-new Mustang parked way out by the art modular? Totally a senior's car. And a beater, half rusted, half spray-painted, all four tires were spares? Dopeheads. You stayed away from those cars. Unless you wanted administration searching your locker during pot busts.

"We exacted justice for you," Vonnie said.

"For me? What are you talking about?"

"You shouldn't be mad. It was all out of love," Cheyenne said, patting me on the shoulder.

"I don't even know what to be mad about," I said, though I was getting there. Whatever they'd done, they were acting totally sketchy about it.

Annie leaned forward. "We told the world what's what."

Vonnie inched forward some more, hitting the brakes in little taps that made us all look like we were moving to the beat of a song only we could hear. The van in front of us took too long to turn and she laid on her horn.

She glanced at me. "You're going to love this, Buttercup. We got him back."

"Him who?"

As if in answer, my phone buzzed again. I glanced down. Kaleb. *Oh, no. They didn't.* I opened the text.

SHAVING CREAM? REALLY? GROW UP.

Things clicked into place. "You shaving-creamed Kaleb's house?" Spraying shaving cream onto someone's window screens was big when we were in junior high. The cream was hard to get out, because it liked to foam up when you washed it, plus it cleaned the screens, so whatever you'd written stood out even after you'd washed it off, and the person who got creamed ended up having to scrub their whole screen. It was a big pain in the butt, which made it hilarious, but we hadn't done it since we were twelve.

The girls burst into laughter once again as the van in front of us finally inched out onto the road toward the school and Vonnie whipped around him and flung her car into the parking lot.

"The front windows at his parents' house," she said between guffaws.

"And we shoe-polished his truck windows," Cheyenne added. "Though we have to give Vonnie most of the credit for that one. She's quite the artist, especially when it comes to drawing penises."

More laughter, during which my throat felt stuck together, it was so dry. It was all seriously funny, true, but I could tell from Kaleb's texts that he was not feeling it. And I couldn't say I could blame him. "You drew penises on his truck windows?"

"She also wrote 'I love dicks,'" Annie said, but she was

laughing so hard she had to pause several times before she could get the word "dicks" out.

"And we wrote 'small penis inside' on his window screens. Nothing major. It will all wash out. Don't look so mad, Buttercup. It was the least he deserved after what he did to you."

"I'm not mad," I said, but my voice felt very small, and my hands were sweating.

I texted Kaleb back: WASN'T ME.

They continued talking, telling me about their mishaps and close calls, and the laughter would not stop and I was getting a headache trying to keep my mouth pulled into a grin like I thought this was the funniest thing ever, all the while hoping Kaleb didn't hate me too much, and knowing that he probably did. Wouldn't I have hated someone if I'd thought they'd done something like that to me?

Finally, as Vonnie pulled into her usual parking space, my phone buzzed for the last time that morning:

PYBKS R HELL.

SEPTEMBER

Message 111
Whoever keeps sending this around needs to stop. I
don't want it on my phone because it's disgusting. I
don't want to see a picture of this girl's boobs every
time I turn my phone on.

Message 112
ur boobs sag lol

Message 113
I wld freakin die if I was ash maynard

Message 114
I FEEL LIKE PUKING EVERY TIME I SEE THIS!

I knew cross-country was the place I was going to miss Kaleb
the most. Running sort of belonged to us, in a way. It was

part of who we were. We met during a 5K, we sat together on the bus to every meet, we ran side by side in practice, racing, and we cheered each other on during competitions. When Coach Igo gave me a hard time for being slow, Kaleb rallied for me. And when I wanted to quit—which was about every other day—Kaleb talked me down. We both had other friends on the team, but we'd built our own little cocoon within those friends, and that was where we hung out the most, just the two of us. When Kaleb went to college, he took with him my biggest reason for wanting to stay on cross-country. Without him it was hot and sticky and I was winded and tired and sick of doing the same sport I'd done since eighth grade.

But with the two of us broken up, it was even worse. Before, I had hoped he'd drive home to see me run in a couple of meets, but now I knew that would never happen. I imagined him stretching out in another field with another girl, a college girl, looking at that girl's shorts as she pulled ahead of him in a race, holding her gym bag for her.

It didn't help that his last text was a threat and he'd sounded so much like he hated my guts. I'd texted him back, telling him that it wasn't me, that someone else must have done it, that I hadn't even known anything about it until I'd heard this morning. He never responded. No way would he believe me; not with the timing of it happening right after our breakup. Even if I could convince him that it was Vonnie, he'd only think I put her up to it. I even called him during lunch period, slipping out the performing arts center doors, where all the smokers hid behind the bushes, but he didn't answer.

Part of me was really angry with Vonnie, even though I knew her heart was in the right place.

In between classes and at lunch, she kept telling me I was too quiet. *I know you're mad, Buttercup,* she'd said, *but you'll get over it, and then you'll thank me. Totally. Come on, admit it. It was hilarious what we did.*

I'd smiled, told her again that I wasn't mad, that it was hilarious, and that I was sad about breaking up with him, that was all. But on the inside I felt like she'd ruined everything, and wished she'd just stayed out of my business.

I dressed in my running clothes and used the bench to stretch my calves, then headed outside into the heat, squinting and shading my eyes with my arm.

"Glad to see you could show up," Coach Igo said, standing at the gym door. "I thought you'd given up on our team. You're late."

"Sorry, Coach," I said. "I've got a lot going on."

She frowned at me. "I can guarantee you the Washington Springs girls' team doesn't have a lot going on," she said. "The only thing they've got going on is practice. First meet's next week. You can't afford to have a lot going on. At this point, I'm not sure if you'll be running against them."

"Yes, ma'am," I said miserably, bracing myself for more punishment. I'd seen Coach Igo make teammates run bleachers for being late, even when they had a good excuse. I had nothing.

She stared me down for a minute longer, then sighed.

"First group took off a few minutes ago. You can run with Adrian, Philippa, and Neesy. We'll gather on the track for a talk when everyone's back."

"Okay," I said, and gratefully ducked into the small cluster of senior girls shifting from foot to foot, gathering their hair up in ponytails, retying their shoes. They were our fastest runners. I'd be huffing and puffing to keep up with them, and Coach knew that. But at least I wasn't running up and down the bleachers until my quads practically burst through my skin. She was definitely going easy on me.

We ran through the parking lot and took a left into the residential neighborhood that surrounded our favorite running trail. It was shaded in the hot weather, like today, and we sweated less there. In a month or so, all those leaves would be dropping to the ground and making the trail soft underfoot. I loved the muted *whup whup whup* sound my sneakers made on it in the fall; as if I weren't running so much as I was bouncing on a cloud.

I let my mind wander as we turned onto the trail, immediately going up a hill that had me sucking wind. Neesy was so fast.

My face slid in and out of the dappled sunlight filtering through the trees, and the strobe effect calmed me, relaxed me. I remembered running over the same stretch of trail with Kaleb last fall, both of us wearing caps and gloves with our shorts and T-shirts. Kaleb's cheeks had looked mottled and his nose had been bright red with cold. His eyes were watering from the wind, the tears streaming back toward his ears.

We'd passed a couple of walkers, a gray-haired man and a woman with a cane. They were bundled up, shuffling slowly along, holding hands. They looked content, like being together was all they'd planned to accomplish that day. We automatically shifted so that Kaleb was behind me to share the trail with them, and then veered back together after we'd passed them.

We ran in silence for so long, both lost in our thoughts, I was surprised when he spoke, between measured breaths.

"So you think...we'll be like that?"

I glanced at him. "Like what?"

He motioned with his gloved thumb over his shoulder. "Like them...the old people."

"Be like them how?...You mean old?"

"No." He stopped, bent over, and put his hands on his knees, puffs of breath crowding around his face. It took me a few strides to realize we were stopping. I went back to him. He stood up and grabbed my hands. "I mean, will we be walking this trail together when we're old? Will we be holding hands? In love like they are?"

I smiled, and it felt like all the blood in my body rushed straight to the center of my chest. Warmth flooded me, and I didn't care about the wind and the cold. I held tight to his hands. "I hope so," I said, and he pulled me in by the waist, halfway lifting me up so that I was barely resting on my toes and he was kissing me, deep and with feeling, our mouths hot against the cold wind around us.

We stayed that way until the footsteps of another group

of runners pounded up on us: guys from the team. "Yo, Kale, get some!" one of them yelled as they stampeded past. Kaleb grinned and rested his forehead on mine as we waited for them to disappear from sight.

"I hope so, too," he said. "Come on, you're shivering, we should get moving."

And we started running again, but what he didn't know was that my shivering had nothing to do with the cold; it was the excitement of being with him, and I couldn't shake it, not even after we'd finished the course and I was standing under a shower so hot and steamy it made my flesh red.

I used to love that memory. I used to cherish it like it was precious. Now I hated it, because remembering it—running on this section of "our trail"—reminded me how much I'd been in love with him. And I was trying so desperately to forget that.

By the time we finished the trail, I was several feet behind Neesy and the others. Coach Igo stood at the fence surrounding the track, shading her eyes with a clipboard, which she brought down and wrote on as we approached. I tried not to look as exhausted as I was, but it was impossible. My lungs ached. My legs ached. My heart ached.

We filed in through the gate and walked around the track to steady our breath. Adrian, Philippa, and Neesy walked shoulder to shoulder, whispering their gossip, leaving me a few steps behind them, as if they'd never noticed I'd been running with them. I didn't care what they had to talk about, not really. But it only made me miss Kaleb more. I would normally have been walking around the track with him.

All the groups were getting back from their runs now. A lot of kids were already taking off their running shoes and sliding their feet into flip-flops, downing Gatorade, goofing off on the bleachers, while Coach Igo stood by the fence writing things on that clipboard and shaking her head disgustedly.

I heard footsteps and moved over to let some of the guys from the boys' team pass.

"Hey, Ashleigh," one of them said when they got next to me. It was Silas, from Kaleb's baseball team. They laughed as they passed.

"Hey, Silas." I pulled the elastic out of my hair, letting it fall to my shoulders in wet, sweaty clumps.

The boy walking next to him—I think he was a sophomore named Kent, but I wasn't sure—snickered into his balled-up fists. Silas got a grin to match his, like he was holding in a great big joke.

"What?" I asked.

"Nothing," Silas said, and this time he couldn't hold it in. He punched Kent in the shoulder and both of them doubled over in laughter. "I didn't recognize you at first."

"Ooo-kay," I said slowly. "Whatever."

They kept walking, passing Neesy and the other girls, knocking into each other and cracking up every few steps. Idiots. Probably thinking it was so funny that Kaleb broke up with me.

But when I rounded the last corner of the track, I noticed

that other guys were looking at me and laughing, too. And so were a couple of girls. I swiped the back of my shorts with my hands, wondering if there was something on them. I ran my hands over my hair, discreetly wiped my nose with my index finger, looked down at myself for a quick once-over. Nothing seemed out of place.

God only knew what Kaleb had told them.

I decided I didn't care what Kaleb had told them. I was going to have to block out all thoughts of Kaleb if I was going to get over him. I finished my cool-down, half-listened to Coach rag us out for being slow, and then headed into the locker room without even giving Silas and his idiot friends another thought.

I showered, dressed, and headed to the field house, where the volleyball team was running suicides, to catch a ride with Vonnie. The coach blew the whistle and, with moans, the girls fell to a stop.

"See you tomorrow night," the coach hollered as some of the team flopped onto the bleachers, others lay down right on the floor, and others, including Vonnie, stormed off toward the doors. "On time, next time!"

Vonnie's hair was falling out of her braid, totally un-Vonnie-like, and her face and chest were glistening with sweat. Her mood seemed positively foul.

"Come on," she said, blowing right past me without slowing down. "Let's get out of this shithole."

She picked up her gym bag and headed for the door.

"I'll wait in the hall while you shower."

"Screw that, I'll shower at home," she growled.

I had a hard time keeping up with her as we went for the car. The whole time, Vonnie railed on about the coach. "She's such a bitch, making us all run because Olivia was late. And it's not like Olivia was fooling around or anything. She was taking a freaking makeup test. It's not right. You should have your dad go all apeshit on her. Fire her fat ass."

"I don't think he's going to do that. Besides, you're not the only one. Coach Igo is mad at me, too," I said. "I was late, so she made me run with the seniors. I thought I was going to die out there on the trail and nobody would know."

"They're both ass-hats. They should form a club."

Vonnie unlocked her car and got in. I piled into the passenger seat, gathering my things into my lap again. "Where are Cheyenne and Annie?"

"They went home with Annie's brother. Didn't come to practice. Smart bitches."

"She'll make them pay for that."

Vonnie snorted. "Yeah, she probably will. Knowing her, she'll make all of us pay for it." She started the car and backed out of the parking space. "Wanna come over? I think Rachel's gonna stop by later."

"Nah," I said. "Not today. I'm kinda bummed."

"Come on, Ashleigh, you have to get over him eventually."

"It's been two days."

"Not really," she said. "You spent a whole summer with

lawn chair butt watching him play his stupid baseball games. You said so yourself. You should be glad to get rid of him."

"You know, it wasn't that long ago you were telling me to send him a picture of myself so he'd remember me while he was at college."

"Um, yeah, I was wasted when I said that."

"Well, I still did it."

"You shouldn't have," she snapped.

We drove in silence, Vonnie navigating the streets toward my house a little faster than usual. I sat next to her and seethed, thinking she wasn't driving fast enough.

Finally, she pulled into my driveway and sighed. "I'm sorry, I'm pissed off from practice. I just meant...you shouldn't have taken it, because you're hurt now. And I hate to see you hurt, that's all."

"No big deal," I said, even though on the inside it was still feeling a little like a big deal. I needed Vonnie to be there for me. To understand how I was hurting inside, whether it was my own fault or not, and make me feel better. And not by "vigilante justice" and insisting that I just get over him, either.

Mom was curled up in the recliner, hunkered over a paperback, her glasses sliding down her nose.

"Hey," she said when I walked in. "You're home late. How was practice?"

I shrugged.

"Uh-oh, what does that mean?"

I went into the kitchen and got a bottle of water out of the refrigerator, hearing the thunk of the recliner footrest closing. Mom came into the kitchen behind me, taking off her glasses. "Hey," she said. "Are you fine?"

I shrugged again. "I don't know. I guess."

Mom's forehead wrinkled. I hadn't said my line—"Frog fur!" or even "Dandy needs a tune-up!"—but I wasn't in the mood to play cute games. She sat at the table and pushed a chair out for me with her foot. "Tell."

I took a long drink of water and slid into the chair next to her. "Vonnie and I kind of had a fight. It's no big deal."

"Oh, you'll make up. You two always do." She bent her head, trying to look into my face. "But there's something else?"

"It's nothing. I'm kind of sick of cross-country. I'm not very good. I'm always having to push myself way harder than everyone else just to keep up."

"It's good to push yourself harder."

"Not if your lungs are about to catch fire. Plus...I don't know...it's not as fun anymore."

She laid her glasses on the table. "Oh, Ashleigh. This is about Kaleb, isn't it? You miss him. I'm sure he'll come see you run."

I glanced up at her, took another drink. "I wouldn't count on that."

"Well, of course you can count on that. He adores you."

"Not since we broke up, Mom. He hates me now."

She looked stricken. I felt even more horrible than before,

seeing how much it shocked and hurt her to know Kaleb was gone from my life, and that I hadn't told her right away. "What happened?" she asked. "You two have been together a long time."

I thought about it. I thought about Holly. My accusations. Our fights. About the photo that started it all. I willed myself not to show it on my face. How could I tell her what had happened? This was totally private, totally not Mom territory. I shrugged again. "It was too hard with him being so far away."

Mom leaned over and wrapped me in a one-armed hug. Her hair pressed up into my nose and I inhaled deeply. It smelled like coconut shampoo and perfume. I had no idea what scent it was that she wore, but it always gave me a safe feeling, a happy feeling, a feeling of comfort.

"Oh, honey, I'm sorry. I know it hurts to break up with a boy you really like."

I closed my eyes, tears threatening all over again. I envisioned my last text from Kaleb, the one where he vowed to pay me back for Vonnie's prank, to try to stave the tears off. "Thanks, Mom, but I'll be okay." I pulled away and picked up my water bottle. "I should do my homework before dinner."

She nodded, gave me a pitying smile, and brushed my hair out of my face. "Give cross-country a chance," she said. "It's probably just that you're missing him. I'd hate to see you quit something you love simply because you're heartbroken right now."

"I know, Mom. You're right," I said, and headed up to my room.

By the time Dad got home, I'd watched a movie on my computer and hadn't even bothered to pick up my backpack or do the homework inside it. I kept going back to that day on the trail with Kaleb, and then staring at the text he'd sent me: PYBKS R HELL. I got angry every time I looked at it. I'd never been anything but devoted to him. He'd broken up with me, not the other way around. I deserved more of a chance than this. He should have believed me when I said I didn't do it. He shouldn't even have had to ask.

Finally, I went down to dinner, where once again Dad was complaining behind the newspaper.

"It's aliiive," he said in a frightened voice when I walked in.

I smiled and gave him a kiss. "Hi, Dad."

"Mom said you broke up with Loverboy." He tipped a corner of the paper down and looked at me over the top. "His loss."

"Thanks."

I wished I could believe that was true. It still felt like my loss.

I never spoke a word during dinner. I zoned in and out of Mom and Dad's conversation, leaving me plenty of time to sit and think.

Kaleb and I were through. But what did he mean by "paybacks are hell"? What was he planning to do? Shaving-cream my window screens? Something worse? Would he use one of his "boys" to get back at me, someone in the school?

I remembered Silas walking past me on the track, laughing with his friend. His words, "I didn't recognize you at first." They didn't make sense. At least to me they didn't. Would Kaleb use Silas to get back at me?

But how?

And then it dawned on me.

The picture. On the day we broke up, Kaleb had said he'd deleted it, but what if he hadn't? All of our fights had started because I thought he'd shown it to Nate. Kaleb knew that one way he could get me back would be to... *What if it got out?*

Oh, no. He wouldn't.

I no sooner had the thought than my phone buzzed in my pocket. I whipped it out and opened the text.

"I thought we said no cell phones at the dinner table," Dad said. "It's rude to have our dinner interrupted by teenage melodrama. And misspelled melodrama, at that!"

He went on, but I stopped hearing him. I stopped hearing anything but the ringing in my ears as I gazed down at the text I'd gotten from Vonnie.

OH SHIT BUTTERCUP BIG TROUBLE.

Attached was a forwarded photo.

A photo of me, full-frontal naked in front of Vonnie's bathroom mirror. Someone had captioned the photo: SLUT UP FOR GRABS!

Mom was saying something to me. I looked up at her, but it was like looking at a stranger. My brain was so jumbled I couldn't make sense of where I was or who was talking to me.

"...your phone away until after dinner..."

But the words made no sense. All my brain could take in was *slut up for grabs slut up for grabs slut up for grabs.*

"I'm sorry," I said. "I've got to call Vonnie. It's an emergency."

I didn't wait to hear my mom's response. I laid down my fork and pushed away from the table, racing upstairs, trying not to vomit or to let my trembling hands drop the phone, only one thought going through my mind:

If Vonnie had seen the photo, who else had?

I dialed Vonnie's number as I rushed toward my bedroom. "Oh my God, that bastard" was the way she answered her phone.

"Where did you get it?" I felt dizzy and wondered if it was possible for a body to forget breathing altogether and drop dead on the spot.

She paused for a minute. "I'm sorry, Buttercup."

"What? Where did you get it? Did Kaleb send it to you?"

Another pause. Then, "No. Chelsea Graybin sent it to me."

For a moment, nothing made sense. Chelsea Graybin didn't even know Kaleb, did she? "Wait. Chelsea Graybin the cheerleader? How did she...?"

"I'm pretty sure someone else sent it to her. Cheyenne and Annie and Rachel all got it, too."

My legs gave out and I fell back on my bed. It was like Vonnie's words were bouncing off me like hail. I heard them, I felt them, but they didn't sink in. They couldn't. Panic rose up in my throat.

"You there?" Vonnie was saying, and I was nodding, staring out into space, the magnitude of what this meant slowly sinking in. "Ash? Hello?"

"Oh my God," I finally squeaked out. "This was what he meant by payback. He hadn't sent it before, but now... Oh my God. What am I gonna do, Vonnie?"

"I don't know. Just let it ride, I guess."

"Let it ride? I'm naked!"

"But people forget stuff really fast. Look, people will probably talk about it for a couple days but won't even remember it by next week."

Talk about it. God, everyone would be talking about it. Images of the track pressed in on me again. Silas and Kent walking by, laughing. *I didn't recognize you at first.* Of course, it made sense now. I had clothes on. He almost didn't recognize me because I had clothes on. He'd already seen it. All the kids over on the bleachers talking, giggling. How many of them had seen it? Had everyone seen it? Had everyone seen me naked? Were they all calling me a slut, making fun of me right in front of me?

The dinner I'd eaten sloshed around in my belly and I lay back on my bed, squeezing my eyes shut to keep from being sick.

"Listen, try not to..." But Vonnie trailed off. Even she

didn't know what to say. I never thought I'd see the day that Vonnie Vance would be struck mute. This was bad. Worse than bad.

"I've got to go," I finally said. "My dad will be freaking out that I haven't come back down for dinner. He'll take away my phone." And for some reason, it seemed really important to me that I keep my phone. Like I didn't want to miss anything, no matter how bad it was. "Don't forward it to anyone, okay?"

"I can't believe you'd even think I would!"

"No, you're right. I don't. Will Cheyenne and Annie? Or Rachel?"

"I don't think so. Why would they? Don't worry about it, Buttercup. At least you look good in it."

If only I could find consolation in that.

I hung up and leaned back against my pillows. My hands were shaking. I was totally on edge. And totally angry. How could Kaleb, who'd been telling me a week ago that he loved me, who'd once promised he wanted us to grow up to be a cute little old couple together, who'd asked me to prom with cupcakes, do this?

He'd never given me a chance to explain that I hadn't been the one to write those things on his windows. He'd never even listened to what I had to say. He only wanted to get back at me. And even as payback, this was a pretty hateful thing to do to someone.

I didn't expect him to answer, but I called him anyway.

To my surprise, it only rang once.

"Leave me alone," he said.

"So guess what just got texted to me?"

He chuckled. Chuckled! I wanted to hit him. "Wow, that traveled fast."

"Wasn't that your goal?"

"My goal was to make you stop being psycho and leave me alone. It didn't work, apparently, because here you are calling me again. It's kind of pathetic."

"Who did you send it to?"

"Just some people in my contacts list."

"All of them?"

"No. Not my mom." Again, he laughed. My heart sank even lower. Right now, I hated him so much it felt like something molten boiling through me.

"How could you do this to me, Kaleb? I wasn't even with Vonnie when she wrote those things. I didn't know anything about it until this morning. I never would have done anything like that to you."

"Yeah, okay, whatever, Ashleigh."

"It's true! I didn't ask her to do it!"

I heard keys jingling in the background and the slam of his truck door. He was going somewhere—going on about his night like nothing had ever happened. "Look, the point is to leave me alone. Don't text me, don't call me, don't think about me. And don't have your friends do shit to my parents' house or my truck. That's all. Just leave me alone. And don't send me any more of your skanky pictures, either."

"That picture was only meant to be seen by you."

"Well, that was your mistake."

And he hung up.

I flung my cell phone across the room. It bounced off the closet door and landed on the floor. No sooner had it landed than it buzzed again. I squeezed my eyes shut tight and tried to take a deep breath, but every time I attempted to suck in air, I could feel angry tears pushing behind my eyelids, fighting and punching to get out. I hated Kaleb. How could I ever have thought I loved him?

"Ashleigh!" I heard from downstairs. My dad was calling. "This is enough. Come finish dinner." I had no idea how I was going to go downstairs and eat broccoli and listen to my dad's school board problems when I knew I had a huge problem of my own brewing.

Slowly, I got up and made my way to my phone. I picked it up and it buzzed again. Two text messages. One was the same photo, sent from Cheyenne, which made me wince. Was she being a friend and warning me, or had she simply forwarded the photo to everyone in her contacts list?

Slut up for grabs!

The second was from a number I didn't even recognize. All it said was: GROSS. SLUT.

DAY 22

COMMUNITY SERVICE

I was almost done with my research. Even if I hadn't had the starring role in *Ashleigh Maynard: The Slut Chronicles*, I now knew everything there was to know about my own case, including all the rude, opinionated things people say about issues they know absolutely nothing about. Almost every online news story about the Chesterton High School sexting scandal had comments on the bottom of it. Stuff that would have made me cry if I hadn't already gotten used to being beat up on by people I didn't know.

People called me a whore. They said my mom and dad were horrible, lazy parents, and that I shouldn't ever have been left alone with my cell phone. They said I was a bad influence and that I was an example of everything that was wrong with the world today. They said I was lucky I wasn't pregnant or dead of some disease by now. That I had low self-esteem and that I was a poster child for eating disorders. They said I should get punished. Many thought my community service wasn't punishment enough, not by a long shot.

And that was nothing compared to what they said about Kaleb.

I also knew everything there was to know about a similar case that happened to a girl in Florida, who sent naked photos of herself on a dare, and another girl in Alabama, whose story was eerily similar to mine.

I had all the websites memorized, had studied facts and figures, knew statistics and definitions. Had it all down pat. I was a sexting expert, though I would argue that I was already one of those the very minute I got the first text from Vonnie with my naked picture attached.

Now all that was left was to start designing my pamphlet, and I had sixteen hours to do that.

In a way, that made me sad. Not that I loved having my every afternoon filled with community service, but there was something I didn't mind about sitting next to Mack, sharing candy and listening to music and, most importantly, not having to talk about what had happened to me. It was safe here.

In some ways, Mack had turned into my new best friend.

Not that Vonnie and I hated each other or anything, but we'd definitely grown apart. Which is easy to do when one of you is eating Tootsie Pops on a bus heading to a volley-ball game and the other of you is eating Tootsie Pops with a juvenile offender heading toward the end of court-ordered community service. We'd drifted, that was the best way I could put it.

It was odd when I thought about it. Vonnie and I had both lost the same thing: me. I'd lost myself when Kaleb sent that photo to his friends. Or maybe it was when we broke up. Or it could have been when I started to fear los-ing him over the summer. Vonnie had lost me when all the trouble went down and I became the biggest story Chester-ton High School had ever known. But even though we'd both lost the same thing, her life really hadn't changed much at all. Only mine had. She was going on as always. I was floundering.

Darrell had finished his community service hours, but he hadn't completed his project yet. His biggest problem was that he couldn't spell, so everything took him ten times longer than it did the rest of us. Mrs. Mosely had signed off on his paper and we'd told him good-bye, but he surprised us all by showing up day after day and going right to his computer, even though he no longer had to.

"I want to finish this," he'd said to Mrs. Mosely. "I never did nothing like this before and I want to see how it turns out."

Mrs. Mosely didn't mind, and she pulled her chair up next to his some days and helped him with his spelling. And when she wasn't around, we all helped him. He would yell out when he got stumped and we would call the answers back to him.

All except Mack, who, typically, really didn't say anything.

Meanwhile, my dad's whole life had become meeting after meeting. Forget Superintendentman out saving the world; he was busy enough just trying to save his job. He was rarely home in time to read the paper in his lounge pants before dinner. Half the time he wasn't home for dinner. But sometimes that was a relief. On the nights he had to go to a late meeting, I walked home, glad to not be in his car trying to figure out how to fill the void where conversation used to be. I loved my dad, and I felt insanely guilty about what was happening to him, but I didn't know how to say those things. I didn't know how to talk to him at all.

It was a surprisingly warm evening when I left room 104 after completing my forty-fourth hour. The fall chill had lifted for what we all figured was the last time before winter rolled in, so I was kind of happy to be walking, even if I still felt really self-conscious every time a car rolled past. Did the person inside recognize me? Had they seen the photo? Those were the thoughts that repeated in my brain.

I pushed through the glass double doors into the fresh air and found Mack unwrapping a Starburst outside.

"I ate all mine," I said.

He popped a yellow one into his mouth. "Greedy," he said around it.

"You got any pink left?" He rolled his eyes and acted all

put out but dug into his pocket and came out with a hand-ful. I took a pink one off the top. "My favorite."

We started down the sidewalk, side by side, chewing our candy.

"You walk home every day?" I asked, mostly because I'd never seen him out on the sidewalk before. Usually he either left through the downstairs side door or was still at his computer when I called it a day.

"Not really," he said. "I'm not going home right now."

"Where you going?"

"Nowhere exciting."

"I'm coming with you."

He swallowed, considered me, and said, "You got a few minutes?"

"Sure."

I followed him down some side streets, at first headed toward my neighborhood but then veering off to the south, over to where the smaller houses were. Some of them were run-down, and as we kept walking, I noticed that a few were boarded up and others had tons of junk lying around in their yards—old, broken toys and beat-up appliances. Chesterton wasn't a very big city, so I knew these houses existed. I knew there were poorer kids in our school, but we stayed pretty separate most of the time. Kids from my neighborhood never really had any reason to go to this area, and vice versa.

"You live over here?" I asked as we turned the corner onto a dead-end street.

"Used to."

We walked to the end of the street, past a house with an overgrown yard and a shutter that was hanging askew. The lot on the other side, obscured by a dilapidated RV that someone had parked on the street, had been converted into a skateboarding park. The park looked as if it hadn't been used in a long time.

Worn brown ramps of various shapes and sizes jutted up into the sky, their faces chipped and spray-painted with graffiti. Dandelions grew in the cracks of the pavement between the ramps, and the rails were rusted almost through. Mack headed for a ramp and ran up to the top of it, his shoes sliding on its smooth surface. I stood on the pavement and looked up at him as he turned and sat with his legs stretching down the ramp.

"This is where you were taking me?" I asked.

"Don't be a snot. Come up," he answered.

I thought about it for a second, then dropped my backpack to the ground and tried to walk up the ramp. I didn't make it and laughed as I slid backward down to the blacktop on my knees.

"You've gotta run at it," he called down. "You can run, right?"

I gave him a sarcastic head-tilt, my hands on my hips. "Har har, yes I can run. I do it every day of my life." *Well, used to*, a voice inside my head corrected, but I batted it away. I backed up a few steps and ran at the ramp, barely making it to the top, scrabbling with my fingers to get some traction. When I finally did, I pulled myself to standing and brushed my hands off dramatically. "See? I can do it."

He applauded, then reached into his pocket and handed me another pink Starburst. "Your reward," he said.

I sat next to him and let my legs hang down over the ramp next to his. From up here you could see as far as the high school, hay bales dotting the pastures between the skate park and the football field. "I had no idea this place even existed," I said.

"That's because everyone skates over at Mulberry Park. Nobody comes here anymore. The weeds." He gestured at a patch of grass poking up right at the bottom of one of the ramps. "There's a creek back here, too." He pointed off into the woods that created the dead end.

"Do you skate?"

He shook his head. "Nope, never. My dad used to bring me here when I was little and we did this sometimes, though." He leaned back and pulled off his shoes, setting them next to him on the top of the ramp. His socks, which were a grungy off-white color, were loose and thin. He tugged them up, then stood, held his arms out at his sides as if he were surfing, bent his knees, and slid down the ramp on his feet. At the bottom, he turned, grinning at me from beneath his curly, unkempt bangs. "Try it."

I shook my head. "I'll kill myself."

"Seriously, if I can do it, you can do it. Just try."

I stared at him, then shook my head and kicked off my shoes, placing them on the ramp, next to his. "If I end up with a broken leg, you're going to have to carry me to the hospital," I said.

"So don't break your leg."

"Fine." I got up and stood at the top of the ramp, which looked a whole lot steeper now that I was getting ready to slide down it. How did anyone get the courage to do this on a skateboard?

"Bend your knees," Mack coached. "And lean forward a little bit. And don't go over that torn-up chunk or you'll fall."

"Stop talking," I said, and inched forward. "Okay. Okay."

"Do it, you weenie!" he called out, and I flinched.

"Stop it, you're going to make me fall!" I cried, but we were both laughing. At last I put my foot down on the ramp and leaned into it, then slid all the way to the bottom, falling backward onto my rear at the very last minute. "Ha! I did it!" I said as Mack pulled me to standing.

"Good job. Now try that one," he said, pointing to a taller ramp across the pavement. "If you're such a pro." He trotted over to it, and after a slight hesitation, I followed.

Up and down the ramps we slid, our socks getting black on the bottoms and our legs getting tired from running up the ramps with no traction. It was the most fun I'd had in a long time, and I loved the feeling of doing something dorky and stupid without having to worry about any sort of fallout. Finally, physically spent, we crawled back to the top of the shorter ramp and hung our legs over the side like we'd done when we first arrived, only now breathing heavy and shedding our jackets.

We were silent for a minute, gently tapping the backs of our legs against the ramp and making little *thump thump thump* noises with our heels. "So, you almost done with community service?" he asked, breaking the silence.

"Sixteen hours."

"Bet you'll be glad to get done. You got a raw deal. No way they should have busted you like they did."

"They wanted to make an example out of me," I said. "They supposedly went easy on me, though."

"Who's they?"

And suddenly I was desperate to tell someone about everything that had happened to me. I hadn't told Vonnie or Cheyenne or Annie or anyone about those horrible days when I found out how big the whole scandal had gotten. I'd been so embarrassed and frightened and alone, and I'd wanted to keep it to myself—not that any of them were really asking, anyway. But now I wanted someone to know.

So I told Mack about the parents who'd pressured Principal Adams, the same ones who'd called the police, the same ones who were quoted in the newspapers, demanding action from the DA.

I told him about my first meeting with the police. How freaked out I had been as I walked into the police station.

The police were nice about it, and, as scared as I was, I felt grateful. At least they didn't handcuff me, they didn't yell at me, they didn't lock me up in a dirty cell—all the things I'd been frightened they'd do.

The officer had taken us into the meeting room and told us to have a seat. Mom's eyes had been red and swollen, and Dad had that same grim, stoic look that he'd had so often by that time. One that looked like he was holding in a mouthful of marbles or chewing on something unpleasant and dangerous.

I'd sat down between them, across the table from the officer, whose hair was slicked back and perfectly combed, like a game show host's.

"That was the first time it really occurred to me," I told Mack.

"What?" Mack asked.

"That I'm a criminal. I mean, I'm used to it now, but that day was the first time it hit me. I never thought I'd, like...be questioned by a cop, you know?"

He shrugged. "I guess. But it's not like you were out robbing banks or something."

"I know," I said. "It's not the same. But still...the way the cop talked to me..."

And I went on to tell him about how the police officer had folded his hands together on top of the table when we got settled, and then had gotten all toothy smile on us and told us that they were going to go easy on me because I didn't mean to be an offender.

I told Mack about how when the officer said they were going to work with me, Dad boomed, "Work with her? You

.

call dragging her here and grilling her working with her? She took a damned picture, and she's scared to death. Look at her. Child pornography. That's bullshit. Kids are pulling this shit all the time and you know it." And how I'd been thankful to my dad for saying that, even though I wasn't so sure he really believed it.

And I told Mack how the officer used my name too many times and how he talked down to me like I was stupid and how I felt like I was about an inch tall when I had to admit in front of my parents that I'd been drunk when I took the photo and that Kaleb had liked it at first and that I knew he'd liked it because we'd made out all day afterward.

Mack didn't say anything while I talked. He sat there, looking out toward the high school, thumping his legs against the ramp, nodding every now and then or making a disbelieving noise, but not interrupting, just letting me talk. Letting me tell the story and get it all out.

I finished by telling him how the officer wrote a bunch of things in my file, then closed it and tapped it a few times on the table. How he gave a smile, like everything was good, and said, "Thank you, Ashleigh, for cooperating. We'll be in touch."

And I told Mack the worst part—how when the officer left the room, it felt much larger, much barer, much more open in his absence, and how I'd shivered and wrapped my arms around myself, feeling stupid and humiliated and alone.

"Your parents were there, though, so it's not like you were alone," Mack said.

I nodded. "I know," I said. "I wasn't technically *alone* alone, but"—I paused—"but I ruined something." That was the best way I could put it. I'd ruined something with my parents, because before this I'd never really done anything wrong. We'd had our occasional arguments, but I'd never really done anything to disappoint them before. Not like this.

Since this had happened, they had been focused on how it affected them. It seemed a little unfair. I was the one in trouble. I was the "sex offender." It seemed like there was a "me" and a "them" now; not an "us."

By the time I finished talking, the sky had darkened and the streetlamps had come on, bathing Mack and me in an orange glow. The spray paint on the ramps took on a peculiar brightness, the concrete at their bottoms black pools.

I waited for Mack to say something. To open his mouth and speak. What I really wanted was for him to share his story now, to tell me how he'd ended up in Teens Talking and what his project was about. But when he finally opened his mouth, the only word that came out was "Sucks."

"Yeah," I said. "It does." And then more silence stretched between us, and part of me felt like he was expecting me to say something more, but I'd told him everything. Or at least everything I was willing to tell. And he'd told me nothing, as usual. And he wasn't going to. So I finally gathered myself up and said, "I probably should go."

"Yeah, me, too," Mack answered.

I put on my shoes, then stood and sideways-walked down the ramp and picked up my backpack. I glanced at

Mack, who was tying his shoes. "Next time show me the creek?"

"Sure," he said, without looking up.

I headed back home, thinking about how, even though Mack hadn't told me his story, he'd at least listened to mine. In some ways, my step felt lighter for having told it. I just hoped I didn't end up regretting it.

SEPTEMBER

Message 174
Is it true ur up for grabs? Cuz I'll grab!

I told my mom that I needed to retake a test before school, so she dropped me off on the way to work and I was there before anyone else. For some reason, this seemed like the safest bet to me. If I was going to try to fly low and incognito, like Vonnie suggested, the best way would be not to make a grand entrance.

I took my books to the library and studied under the flickering fluorescent lights, trying to keep my mind off my cell phone.

It had buzzed all night long. Part of me wanted to turn it off, make it stop, but another part of me—the humiliated part—knew that the messages were happening no matter if my phone was off or on. If they were going to be sent, I wanted to at least be in the know. In some ways I couldn't tear myself away from them, no matter how much they hurt to read. So I left the phone on, a piece of me sinking lower and lower every time the alert sounded. Message after message after message. Vonnie, trying to comfort me, trying to tell me that nobody would care. Friends asking what the hell happened, asking if it was faked, asking why I did it.

And the unfamiliar numbers. Those were the worst. Those were the ones calling me a slut and making disgusting suggestions about what I should be doing in future pictures. I guessed that some of those might have come from Kaleb's friends, and maybe even some from Holly or whoever the hell he was with now.

At first I had read them all, even answered some of them, but after a while I'd given up. I read them and deleted them, and then eventually started deleting them without reading. I hoped that at least someone out there had done the same thing with my photo: deleted it.

The closer it got to the first bell, the more on edge I got. My foot twitched on the floor uncontrollably. My hands shook. That ringing in my ears came back. And as students began to trickle into the library, handing in books, passing through, I felt more and more like I was rooted to my chair. I would never be able to get up and walk to class. I wasn't strong enough.

But soon—way quicker than I wanted it to be—Mrs.

Dempsey, the librarian, came by with a handful of books and said, "Class starts in three minutes."

I closed my book and stood on weak legs, peering out into the hallway through the library windows. Everything looked normal. Nobody seemed to be scandalized out there. Maybe Vonnie was right and this was nothing. Maybe nobody would say anything at all.

I gathered my things and slithered out of the library, hurling myself into the stream of students, looking nowhere but straight ahead. I put one foot in front of the other, hoping to get to my destination without incident.

I turned the corner, bypassing my locker, heading to the science wing.

And that was where Nate was standing, with Silas and Danny Cross. Danny had his arm slung around the neck of his girlfriend, Taylor, whose friend Jenna was standing on the other side of her.

Silas saw me and, as if in slow motion, a knowing grin spread across his face and he bumped Nate's biceps with his elbow. Nate's head jerked up and our eyes met, and he let out a bark of laughter, bending at the waist and covering his mouth with his palm like douchebag guys do when they want everyone to look at them. Like an animal herd, the whole group snapped to attention, their heads popping up, their faces at first curious and then turning to disgust, or hate, or laughter.

I swallowed and kept walking, pretending I couldn't see them. *Blind. I'm blind. I don't see this.*

"Hey, Ashleigh," Silas called. "You look good today. Something's different, though. What is it?" Against my will, I turned toward him, just in time to see him tapping his chin in mock-serious thought, like he was the damn *Thinker* or something. He snapped his fingers. "Oh! Dude! I know what it is! You got your hair cut. No, no. That's not it."

I narrowed my eyes at him, but even I could feel that my will wasn't really behind it. I was going for hateful but was probably only achieving fearful beggary. *Please don't say anything, please don't say anything.*

"Nah, she got contacts," Nate said.

"No, it's something bigger than that. Something I can't quite put my finger on..." Silas cupped his hands in front of his chest like he was holding on to a pair of breasts, and Nate and Danny were practically drooling all over themselves with laughter. A few more people were pausing to gape at what was going on, and despite the fact that I was trying so hard to be blind to them, I could still see what they were doing, the way they laughed, the way they leaned their heads together to talk. I forced my legs forward, willing them to go faster, faster. All I had to do was get around them and through the doorway of my science class right on the other side. It was the same as ignoring the pain at the end of a really long run, I tried to tell myself.

"Oh! I know what it is!" Silas finally boomed, and his words felt like shrapnel landing on me. "You have clothes on! That's totally why I didn't recognize you."

Don't hear it, Ashleigh, I told myself. *Be blind and deaf to it. Exist in your own quiet, dark world. You're in a tunnel. You're floating. Just a few more feet and you're there at the finish line.*

But as I passed Danny, Taylor looked over her shoulder and said, so quietly it was almost not there at all, "Slut."

Her friend Jenna nodded in agreement. "Skank."

And the looks on their faces were not of cruelty, but of such disappointment—like they'd expected me to be better than that—I wanted to fall on the floor and cry. I wanted the door at the end of the hall to open up and suck me out into a tornado, spit me out in another school, where nobody had a clue who I was. Taylor had been on cross-country last year. We'd shared a bag of M&M'S on the way home from one of our meets. She'd been in my Algebra II class. She'd always been so nice.

She'd always been so nice.

Way too nice to ever stand, drunk and naked, in front of a bathroom mirror and take a picture of herself. Way too nice to send that picture to her college-bound boyfriend. She would never even have entertained the idea.

And something about that knowledge made me feel all the more humiliated. Because I had thought I'd be too nice to do something like that, too. But obviously I wasn't nearly as nice as I'd thought I was.

Just be blind. Don't see their faces. Don't hear their words. Be in the dark. Bottom-of-a-well dark. Lost-in-a-forest dark.

Somehow I made it into my science classroom, and

somehow I endured the whispering I heard around me while Mr. Kenney, clueless, wrote notes on the board. Somehow I kept from crying when Tyler Smart held up his cell phone and the people around us snickered as my breasts, my belly flashed across the tiny screen.

And I made it down the hallway again, just me, just blind and deaf Ashleigh, just floating Ashleigh, to my English class, and somehow I didn't throw up in ceramics class when my table partner, Phillip, kept molding boobs into the sides of the bowl he was making, joking that he was going to call his piece *Ode to Maynard*.

Somehow I made it through until lunch.

Vonnie and Cheyenne were sitting at our usual table, hunched over a shared plate of Tater Tots, when I got there. I was in a horrible mood and wasn't certain that I was going to be able to make it through the rest of the day. I was pretty sure I wouldn't make it through without crying. Someone had grabbed my butt when I'd leaned over to stuff my backpack into my locker, someone had called me a whore when I'd walked past one of the lunch tables, and I'd had enough. I didn't want to be touched or called names. I didn't deserve to be treated that way.

I grabbed a pudding cup from the mobile cart and flopped down next to Vonnie. Cheyenne didn't look up from her lunch, and probably I was being too sensitive, but something about the way she was ignoring me felt like the last straw. If I couldn't count on my friends to act normal, how could I expect anyone else in the school to act that way?

"What? Should I sit somewhere else?" I snapped.

Cheyenne's eyes went wide. "What?"

I pulled the foil off my pudding. "You look embarrassed."

"Oh," she said, and flushed. She bent her head low and stuffed a Tater Tot into her mouth. "I'm not," she said around the Tot.

Rachel and Annie sauntered over with trays of pizza and sat down across from Cheyenne. They were talking quietly together. And as much as I wanted to have a normal lunch—at least have that much in this horrible day—I couldn't keep the upset that had been filling me up all day from spilling over.

"So, Rachel," I said, "I have been meaning to thank you."

She turned toward me, and I noticed that neither of them—actually, nobody at the table—looked particularly happy. She raised her eyebrows.

"That idea you had about sending Kaleb a photo of myself was a really great one." I gave her a thumbs-up and a cheesy grin.

Annie blinked a few times, chewing. She opened her mouth to say something, then closed it again. Rachel just kept eating, didn't say anything.

We all ate in uncomfortable silence, and all I could hear in the mumbling and murmuring surrounding me was my name. I didn't know if it was really there or not, but I heard it. And I wondered how long this would go on—me hearing my name murmured over and over—before I went insane.

Finally, Vonnie leaned over and swallowed the Tater Tot in her mouth. "Everyone is talking about it. In all my classes. Has it been bad?"

"Only if you consider being called a slut a thousand times bad," I said. "But, hey, it'll all blow over, no big deal, right, Von?"

She held out her palms at me. "Whoa, Buttercup, you better cool your shit. I'm trying to be supportive here."

"Well, I appreciate your support," I said, my tone caustic. I knew I was lashing out at the wrong people, but I couldn't help myself. I was so frustrated and hurt and determined not to let it show. I would not cry. I would not react. I would will this to blow over. But I was so close to exploding, I could feel my skin vibrating under my fingernails. I wanted to stand up on the table and yell, *It was just a mistake!* But I also wanted to crawl under the table and die. Mostly, I just wanted the day to be over.

"I got the text like ten times," Rachel said. She still didn't look up from her pizza.

"Me, too," Cheyenne said. "Somebody added your name and phone number to some of them, Ash." She glanced up at me. I held my pudding-filled spoon in midair between the table and my mouth. So that was how I was getting all those texts from unknown numbers.

"Who would do that?" I gasped. I could feel tears prickling the corners of my eyes, and I blinked rapidly to keep them inside. *Do not cry, Ashleigh, do not cry. You are a raisin, you are shriveled and dried up, and your eyes have no tears.*

"I just figured you'd want to know," Cheyenne said quietly. "I think pretty much everybody has gotten the text by now."

"I heard that some kid in the junior high is showing it around," Annie said. "I don't know if that's true, though. Like, who would send it to a junior high kid? That's gross."

I dropped my spoon back into my cup, not hungry at all anymore. "Oh my God," I said, resting my forehead in my hands. "Oh my God."

Vonnie put her hand on my arm. "Don't freak out. It'll be okay."

"That's so easy for you to say," I moaned into my palms. I felt hot, a trickle of sweat coursing down my back. "It's not you who everyone has seen naked. I can't believe Kaleb did this to me."

"Even my brother didn't send his slutty girlfriend's picture around, and he was, like, so proud of that thing," Rachel added. "He told everyone in the world about it, but he didn't show it to anyone."

I glared at her. It had never been clearer to me how much I couldn't stand Rachel. Not to mention how much I didn't see how Vonnie could like her. When Rachel talked about the texts, she almost seemed excited. Like on the inside she was thrilled this had happened to me so she had something to dish about. "Could we not talk about your brother's slutty girlfriend right now? That's what got me into this mess. Thanks to you, everyone is calling me slutty now."

Rachel licked her lips. "Look, I know you're having a

bad day, but just so you know, you're not alone. Do you have any idea how many times I've been asked today if we do it, girl-on-girl? Do you know how many times I've been asked to send a picture of myself around? You're the one who decided to go all full frontal, and I'm paying for it."

"Oh, so I'm supposed to feel sorry for you now?" I said, incredulous. "It was your stupid idea in the first place, Rachel. Do you really think what you're going through is anywhere near the humiliation I'm going through?"

Rachel was definitely the type of person who would think that. She would totally adopt my humiliation if that was what it took to get some sympathy from someone. But I wasn't going to let her. So somebody had asked her a rude question. Poor baby. It was the broken acrylic all over again. Her whole life was one big snapped-fingernail meltdown.

"I didn't think you'd actually do it," she said, and again her lips curved upward, like she was enjoying this. "And besides, I thought you'd just flash your boobs or something. Not get totally naked. It's really embarrassing."

I got up and grabbed my pudding cup. "Well, I'll make this easier on you, then, Rachel. I'll leave. You don't have to be associated with me anymore."

"Buttercup..." Vonnie said, but I ignored her. I wheeled around and marched out of the lunchroom, tossing my trash into the garbage bin on my way out. It landed against the side of the bin and slopped pudding up onto the cafeteria wall. But I didn't care. All I cared about was getting some alone time.

I stormed down the hall and out the front door. I sat on a bench in the sun until the bell rang for fifth period to begin, trying hard to let the stress melt off of me. But I was so tense I felt coiled, ready to spring. I was physically unable to calm down. On some level, I knew my embarrassment wasn't Rachel's fault for suggesting I take the picture, or Vonnie's for pissing Kaleb off. But it felt easier at that moment to blame them, if for no other reason than to have someone in this mess with me, just so I wasn't alone in my mistake.

I stood, turned to face the school. Listened to the hoots and calls of lunch-recharged students as they bounded up and down the stairs, wove in and out of crowds, slammed locker doors. They were all energized again. Plenty of oomph for a new round of Call Ashleigh Names.

I couldn't do it.

I wasn't blind.

Or deaf.

I could see and hear everything.

I turned around and walked home.

"Are you sick?" Mom had poked her head in my bedroom door. She was still wearing her sunglasses. "The school called to say you missed fifth, sixth, and seventh periods."

I didn't answer. Didn't move. Just lay there, facedown, my cheek pressed into the folds of my pillow, staring out the window across my bedroom. Somewhere, hidden in the gloss of the window, there was a heart with Kaleb's and my initials written in it. I'd drawn it in some condensation on the glass one night last winter while talking to him on the phone. When it got cold again, the heart would reappear, a ghost of the past sent to taunt me.

I was no longer pretending to be blind or deaf. Instead, I was frozen. Laid out on a slab of ice, like in a morgue. I was stuck there. I couldn't move.

Mom opened the door a little wider. "You need a chuck bucket?"

"Just a bad day," I mumbled, my cheek scratching against the pillow. Getting frostbitten. Turning black and dying. "Sorry I left without asking."

She sighed and I heard her purse hit the floor; a jangling of car keys. "Is this about Kaleb?"

I didn't answer. I didn't know how. Yes, it was about Kaleb, but not like she thought. I wasn't simply heartsick over a boy. This was much, much worse than that.

"Okay," she said, almost to herself. "Listen, we can talk while we fix dinner. Come down in fifteen minutes?"

"'Kay," I said, though I knew that even if I'd wanted to, I'd never be able to get up and walk down the stairs to help her cook dinner. I thought I almost saw one edge of the heart shape on my window. If I squinted and stared really hard, it was there. I could maybe even see the "K" inside the heart. I glared at it. *Hate you. Hate me. Hate us.*

The phone started ringing downstairs and I heard hurried footsteps and Mom's voice as she rushed to pick it up.

I hated my phone. I never wanted to see it again. I wanted to crush it, to burn it, to run over it with a tank. I didn't care if I never answered another phone as long as I lived.

I heard footsteps coming up the stairs, and then my door opened. Mom stepped through, holding the phone out for me. "It's Vonnie," she said. "Why do you have your cell turned off?"

I tried to shrug, but frozen shoulders don't move, so I just lay there. "I don't know," I said. *I do know but I can't tell you* would have been a much more honest answer.

Mom gave an impatient grunt and tossed the phone on my bed. I felt it thump against my leg when it landed. Damn. I had feeling. "Well, it's off, and Vonnie's trying to get hold of you."

Mom left and I lay there for a moment longer, trying to decide if I could now see the pointy part of the little arrow I'd drawn piercing the heart. I didn't want to.

Then, slowly, slowly, I reached down and picked up the phone, moving as little as I had to, and pressed it between my ear and the pillow.

"Hello?"

"Hey, what's going on? I waited for you after volleyball but you never showed up. And your phone is going right to voice mail."

"I needed some time alone," I said. "And trust me, you wouldn't want to see what happens when my phone is on. It's totally blowing up. Or at least it was last time I checked. I had like a hundred texts."

Vonnie made a sympathetic noise. "Have you talked to him about it yet?"

"Yeah. Sort of. Last night. He couldn't care."

"What a jerk. I can't believe he did this to you. I mean, I always thought he was stuck-up and selfish, but I didn't think he was this mean."

I closed my eyes; a purple imprint of the window showed up behind my eyelids. I could still see pieces of the heart. I couldn't get away from it. "You and me both," I said. "He was always telling me how much he loved me. Guess we know what a crock of crap that was."

"By the way, I found out who spread it around to everyone. Sarah's little brother, Nate."

Nate. Of course. The one who started the whole thing between me and Kaleb in the first place. *How poetic, Kaleb, you get points.* I would never know for sure if Nate had seen it on the day I sent it or if Kaleb had only told him about it. But Nate had definitely seen it now.

Not that it mattered anymore, anyway. Who cared who saw it and who only heard about it and when? Now everyone had seen it, everyone had heard about it, so why even bother to try to figure out when and how exactly the boy I loved had betrayed me? It only added insult to injury. It only made me feel stupid on top of everything else.

"He must have a lot of numbers in his address book, I don't know," she continued. "Anyway, Stephen and Cody are gonna kick his ass when they come home for fall break."

"Stephen and Cody know?" I remembered the two of

them tossing me in the pool a few hours before I took the photo, and how I'd felt so weightless and carefree at the time. What I wouldn't have given to go back to that night and do things over again. I would have stayed in the pool. I would've soaked up that weightlessness and I would have forgotten about Kaleb completely, let him play his stupid little ball game and enjoyed myself without him.

"Yeah. But don't worry, Buttercup, they're on your side."

Great. Just what I needed. Allies, away at college. So now the photo was going around Chesterton High School, possibly the junior high, and at least two colleges. Very nice. I might as well have put my boobs on a billboard on I-70.

I heard Mom puttering around in the kitchen and slowly pulled myself to sitting. My cheek burned, I'd been smushing it against the pillow for so long. No doubt there was a red mark there. I rubbed it.

"I've got to go, Von. I'm supposed to help my mom make dinner."

"Okay, pick you up in the morning?"

My limbs went cold at the thought of even going to school in the morning. But I had to. There was no way around it. Who knew how long it would take for this to run its course? I couldn't wait it out, if for no other reason than at some point Mom and Dad would know something was up. "Yeah, okay."

I hung up and trudged downstairs to the kitchen.

Mom was still in her work clothes—long denim skirt with an apple appliquéd to one hip, tan crocheted sweater

170

vest over a knit top, feet bare except for panty hose, glasses perched on top of her head like a bird in a nest. She was slamming things around as she worked.

"Hey, Mom," I said tentatively. "Are you fine?"

She gave a single bark of a laugh. "Well, my dandy wants to get up and kick someone's ass," she said, which might have been funny on another day. She produced an onion out of nowhere and slapped it onto the cutting board, then began chopping it. "Some parents think their little angels poop nursery rhymes, I swear."

I pulled a frying pan out of the cabinet and laid it on top of the stove, then dumped the hamburger she had thawing inside it, and crumbled it up with a spatula.

She pointed in my direction with her knife. "I've got a five-year-old who is going to be a delinquent someday, mark my words. But try to tell his mother that he's anything other than perfect, and watch out. That woman is in serious denial."

She poured a handful of chopped onion into the pan with the hamburger and then grabbed a jar of minced garlic out of the fridge and added a heaping spoonful.

"But enough about that," she said, brushing her hands off over the sink while I continued to stir and crumble the meat. "What's up with you?"

"My dandy fell down the toilet," I said, trying to match her joke with one of my own, but I couldn't quite get there. All I could feel was the embarrassment of the photo creeping up on me again. "But I don't really want to talk about it."

Mom came up behind me and rubbed my shoulder.

"Oh, honey, I know it feels like the worst thing in the world right now, but you'll forget about Kaleb soon. Another boy will take your mind off of him."

She was wrong. I'd never forget about Kaleb. Not now. He'd made sure of it. I would forever feel shame in the pit of my stomach every time I heard his name. It would never go away. Mortification this big couldn't. But how could my mom ever understand? I couldn't tell her what had really happened. I could only pretend that she was right—that breaking up with Kaleb was my only problem, and that it wasn't a very big problem at that.

"It's no big deal," I said. "I had a bad day is all."

"Well, I admire your attitude about it," she said. "I remember when I broke up with my first boyfriend. I thought I'd die, and the pain lasted forever. It's okay to have a few bad days. It's expected. You two were close."

You have no idea how close, I wanted to say, and again felt heat creep up my ears. Everyone at Chesterton High had a pretty good idea, though.

"I'll tell the office you were sick so you don't end up with a detention. But next time let me know when you need a mental health day, okay? I was worried about you when the school called and I couldn't get you on your cell."

"Yeah, sorry about that. It was sort of a spur-of-the-moment decision."

"I get that." She leaned over me and peered into the meat mixture. "Stir."

We worked alongside each other for a while. Mom

turned on the little TV that hung from the bottom of one of the cabinets and we watched the news. Every now and then she'd comment on a news story, but mostly we cooked away the stress of the day.

After a while, the front door opened and we heard Dad's briefcase drop to the floor in the den.

"Hello," Mom called out, and his footsteps approached the kitchen. Same routine as every night of my life. Something about that routine comforted me, like no matter what drama was going on at school, home was my oasis from it. I could escape to the kitchen, to fixing dinner with Mom while Dad sat at the table and read the paper. I could count on that, on Mom turning off the TV so they could talk while he read, on Dad griping about work. The routine felt like a hug. Maybe everything would be okay. After all, our routine hadn't changed.

"There she is," Dad said when he came into the kitchen. He leaned over Mom from behind and kissed the top of her head. She whirled around, her food-drippy hands held up in front of her, and smiled at him.

"Here I am," she said. "How was your day?"

He came up behind me and reached over my shoulder to pluck a piece of meat from the pan and stuff it into his mouth. He leaned down and kissed my cheek.

"It was work," he said, leaning against the counter, chewing. "Pretty normal until the end of the day."

"Oh, yeah?" Mom was stirring butter into some peas in a bowl.

"Got a call from Principal Adams, up at the high school," he said, and my arm froze. I tried to make it continue stirring the meat, but it wouldn't move. I glanced at Dad, my throat going dry. "A big brouhaha over cell phones or some such."

The numb feeling drained down my wrist and into my hand. I dropped the spatula into the pan. It tipped backward and clattered to the floor. "Dang it," I said, bending to pick it up.

"Anyway, he got a phone call from a parent or something. I don't know. I didn't have a chance to really talk. I was trying to get out of there. I told him I'd call him first thing tomorrow. Exactly what I want to do—begin my day with a crisis. I wish we could just ban cell phones from those buildings. That would take care of a lot of problems. Those kids don't need them, and they do nothing but cause trouble."

I rinsed the dropped spatula and bent to put it in the dishwasher, sure that I was going to be unable to stand up again. My dad's words were tumbling around in my head like clothes in a dryer. *Principal Adams...parent...phone call...cell phones...*

I hoped against hope that this was about something else. Maybe someone was failing a class because they were too busy texting or something. Maybe someone's cell had been stolen from their locker in PE. Happened all the time.

But, hope as I might, somewhere deep down I knew it wasn't something so simple. Why would the principal call my dad if that was the case? You don't call the superintendent unless you've got a really big, or really unusual, problem.

174

And my problem was both.

"You know anything about a cell phone issue at the high school, Ash?" my dad asked, and I swear my teeth were chattering like a dumb cartoon character's. I took a deep breath and, stalling, acted really interested in something that was going on inside the dishwasher. Finally, I pasted on a smile and stood up.

"Nope," I said as convincingly as I could, though to my own ears it didn't sound convincing at all. "I haven't heard anything."

Liar, liar, liar.

"Huh," he said. "Well, I'm sure tomorrow I'll get to the bottom of whatever it is."

Inside of me, something shriveled into a dead hunk.

Tomorrow.

This wasn't going to blow over tomorrow.

It was only going to get worse.

Because tomorrow my dad would know.

SEPTEMBER

Message 198
I always knew you were a slut

Message 199
Will you marry me? LOL

I didn't really sleep—just tossed and turned all night—but when five-thirty came, I jolted awake in a panic. My stomach clenched in on itself with worry, and I raced to the bathroom and hovered over the toilet. I could hear the shower in my parents' bathroom. My dad was up and getting ready for work.

I turned on my phone and texted Vonnie:

ADAMS CALLED DAD. HE KNOWS.

After a few minutes, during which I about gnawed my whole thumbnail off, she replied:

Not the response I was expecting to get. I opened my laptop, pulled up my email, and found the link Vonnie had sent me. It was for a website that posted naked pictures of random girls shot in ordinary places like parties and grocery stores and bedrooms. I clicked it and gasped.

Right across the top was the photo of me, only it was blown up huge. The page had more than two hundred comments, and I scrolled through them, my mouth hanging open. A lot of people had written things about me.

💬 I thought she'd be a lot hotter.

💬 Dude, what are you talking about? I'd break that in half!

💬 Gross you'd probably get some disease.

💬 She's got a lot of people fooled into thinking she's some goody-goody athlete, but pictures don't lie. She's a whore and I'm so pissed that my boyfriend has this text on his phone.

💬 I've seen better on this website. You should check out Charlotte S. posted about three months ago. She'll blow your mind. This chick can't hold a candle.

💬 I can't believe she did this. I would die before I'd do something like this.

My mouth hung open as I read their words. I couldn't count how many times I was called a slut, or worse. And everybody was talking about how ugly I was, how ugly my body was. And even worse were the comments from people who didn't sound like they went to my school. The ones who were looking because they were enjoying it.

A little moan leaked out of me, and for the first time since this whole thing began, I finally started to cry. It wasn't going to go away. Not at all. This was way too big to fade away.

I shut the laptop and pulled my legs to my chest. I rested my forehead on my knees and cried. People I didn't know, looking at my naked body. People I did know—people in my classes, people I passed in the hallways—some of whom I actually liked, saying horrible things about me online. Oh my God, online. My naked body was online. Like a porn star.

I ran back to the bathroom and hovered over the toilet again. Nothing would come up, and I sat on the floor for a long time, resting my head on the toilet seat and letting the tears drip down onto the knees of my pajama bottoms.

I heard the thunk of pipes as Dad shut his shower off. He'd be coming out soon, smelling lemony like his after-shave and starchy from his freshly dry-cleaned shirt and heading off to work.

I couldn't face him this morning, knowing what he was about to find out.

I went back to my room and changed into my running clothes. It wasn't unheard of for me to take an early-morning run to beat the sun, especially when it was hot outside. Mom and Dad wouldn't think anything of it.

I tied my shoes and jogged down the stairs, hitting the front door as I heard Dad opening the bedroom door down the hall. I slipped out before he could see me.

Back when I was in junior high and hoping to someday make the varsity cross-country team, running was my go-to stress reliever. I would breathe in, slowly and steadily, unplug from my phone and my iPod and my parents and everyone around me and just run. I liked the solitude, the way my breath beat in and out of my body without my even thinking about it. I liked the way it warmed me up, spent me, and left me with a floaty feeling after I was done.

I had a trail that I liked to take that led from the back of our subdivision and through some woods. On the other side of those woods was a strip mall that had everything in it from an auto parts store to a karate dojo to a dance studio and even a thrift shop.

I loved to go into the thrift shop for a halfway-point break and pick around at stuff, weaving in and out of the rooms, trying to imagine who'd first bought that old TV with the bent antenna, or the chipped coffee mug that said I DON'T DO MORNINGS or the beaded sweater or the picture of Jesus. I liked to paw through the clothes and shoes. I liked the musty smell and the flickering lighting and the fat, fuzzy gray cat that lurked around, usually in the tablecloth room.

After ducking out of my house this morning, I hit the street and headed for the trail. It would be too early to go to the thrift shop, but I could look in the window. I could still transplant myself into someone else's life, someone else's story. I needed a new story right now. I needed that post-run floaty feeling.

My feet hit the dew-moistened wood chips in perfect rhythm. Kaleb had shown me how to lengthen my stride so that it felt like walking rather than running. He'd improved my stamina by working with me to keep a cadence in my head. He'd challenged me, but he'd also helped me. And even though I'd been running long before I met him, I was unsure if I could do it without him now.

I breathed in and out, trying to clear my thoughts. No Kaleb. It didn't do any good to think about him, to dwell on how good he once was to me. *Just breathe. Just step. Just run.*

There were two joggers up ahead of me, and I passed them on the left. Two moms pushing strollers, talking more than they were running. Seeing them on the trail made me feel safe, secure. They knew nothing about what was going on with me. There were far more people out there who didn't know than people who did. I just had to remember that.

And remember to breathe. To step. To run.

The path turned and I turned with it, listening to the birds wake up and begin calling. It was one of my favorite parts of a morning run. If you paid attention to the calls of birds—really paid attention to them—you would be surprised by how many there were going on around you all the time. We don't tend to hear them because we're so wrapped up in our own stuff—in being loved, in being right, in being on time or first or loudest or funniest or coolest.

I listened to the birdcalls. They were soothing.

I breathed. I stepped. I ran.

I saw the backs of two boys up ahead and slowed down. I couldn't make out who they were from behind, but they were wearing Chesterton High School sweatshirts.

Just like that my breathing got out of rhythm and I was winded. My step was off. I felt like I was flailing. Even in my woods, my stress reliever.

One of them heard my steps and glanced back at me. He said something to the other and they both looked back. I slowed, slowed, stopped, and bent over, my hands on my knees, sucking in ragged gasps of breath, that vomity feeling in the back of my throat again.

Loud and long, there was a catcall whistle. It felt like it reverberated off the trees. Even the birds went silent for a moment.

I stayed where I was, drinking in air until my breathing slowed, feeling the anxiety creep up my legs, my arms, my chest, into my throat. I wanted to say something. To defend myself. But I couldn't catch my breath. All I could think about was my picture on that website. About my dad making that call to Principal Adams this morning.

After a moment, I straightened, then stood and turned and walked back home.

The stress was still there, but all the fight had been drained out of me.

COMMUNITY SERVICE

Mrs. Mosely had to testify in some court case, so Teens Talking adjourned early. You'd have thought we'd won the lottery, the way everyone carried on when she told us to pack up for the day.

Ordinarily, I'd have been bummed about leaving early. I wanted to be done with community service, and the only way to do that was to have my butt in the chair for sixty hours. No way around it. Every early day off was another day I had to show up.

But the freaky warm front that had rolled in was still lingering, and I wanted to hang out with Mack again. It was comfortable hanging out with him, and—who was I kidding?—I needed a friend.

He took his time moseying out of room 104, so I got

drinks and waited for him by the vending machines, a sweaty soda in each hand.

"What's this?" he asked when I handed one to him.

"To wash down the brownies we ate," I said.

He took the soda and popped it open and we headed up the stairs.

"Also in case you get thirsty on our walk."

He grinned. "We going somewhere?"

"Well, we're not going to waste getting out early on a beautiful day like this, are we?" I pushed open the glass doors and we stepped outside. "It's my turn."

"Turn for what?"

"You took me to your hangout—very cool, by the way—so I thought I'd take you to mine. It's oh, so exciting."

Darryl and Kenzie were waiting for rides to pick them up. It sounded like they were arguing, as usual. We walked past them and hit the sidewalk.

"You're not going to make me go to that Vonnie chick's house, are you?"

I laughed. Normally, I wouldn't have thought twice about bringing someone to Vonnie's house, but things between Vonnie and me had been so off lately I wasn't even positive if I would feel comfortable there anymore. Plus, Mack didn't belong in that world.

"Nope. Better."

"The mall? Are we gonna get manicures?" he said in a high-pitched lispy voice that I guessed was supposed to be his imitation of a girl.

I stopped, hands on my hips. "Do I really look like the manicure type to you?"

"Yes."

"Whatever. Just follow me."

The walk toward my end of town was longer than the walk toward his had been, and we both pointed out places along the way that had some sort of meaning to us—the frozen custard shop where my mom's ice cream addiction got downright embarrassing during the summer, the garage where his dad used to work, the skating rink where each of us had gone to birthday parties as kids.

But after a while, it was just me doing the pointing, and it was clear that we'd crossed some invisible boundary line between our lives.

Finally, we hit the entrance to the trail by my house.

"Ta-da!" I cheered, holding my arms out.

He peered into the woods. "This is why we walked a zillion miles?"

My arms dropped to my sides. "You showed me where you like to hang out. This is where I like to hang out. Well, not so much hang out as work out."

"I don't run."

I rolled my eyes, walked around him, and pushed him from behind. "You don't have to. Just come on. I was a good sport about the defying of death you made me do at the skate park. You can be a good sport here. Plus, there's another place I want to show you."

He resisted at first, digging his feet into the ground, but I put all my force behind him and slowly he started walking, chuckling. "Okay, okay. Let's go."

We walked down the trail, moving to the side to let a couple joggers pass.

"So I told you all about my sordid story. When are you done with your community service?" I asked.

He shrugged. "No idea."

"Don't you have a paper?"

"Not anymore. Mosely kept it."

"Why?"

"I thought this was supposed to be relaxing. What's with all the questions?"

"Okay, suit yourself." A squirrel skittered across our path and darted up a tree. "Why all the mystery?" I asked.

"That's a question."

"A valid one, though, don't you think?"

"Another question. You can't not do it, can you?" He tipped his soda up and then crushed the can in one hand. "Some people just don't have lives that are exciting enough to talk about," he said. "I'm one of them. Where are you taking me, again?"

I pointed at him. "Question!" But then I could see the white brick of the strip mall's back wall, and I gestured to it. "Actually, that's where."

He considered it for a moment. "A mall. I thought you said we weren't going to the mall."

"No, I said I wasn't the type of girl who got manicures. I'm totally down with the mall. Plus, this is a strip mall. It doesn't count in the mall world."

"Oh, goody, shopping," he said in that high-pitched voice again, this time hopping on his toes a little and flapping his hands at his shoulders, his curls bouncing. The motion looked so un-Mack-like I couldn't help cracking up.

"Come on," I said, gripping his sleeve and pulling. "Just trust me."

We walked around the building and I led him into the thrift store.

"This is where I really like to hang out," I said. I plunged into the racks and started rifling through the clothes.

He picked up the sleeve of a purple top and let it drop again. "Why?"

"I don't know." I pulled out a shirt and held it up to myself, then put it back. "I guess I kind of like that you never know what the story is behind the things here. Like this shirt." I picked up a T-shirt that had a glittery iron-on appliqué. It read I'M THE FAVORITE. "Somebody bought this shirt because it had meaning to them. And we'll never know what that meaning was, because we'll never know the whole story. I think that's cool." I made a face and slid the shirt back onto the rack. "Probably dumb, though, huh?"

"No, I get it," Mack said. He pulled out a black sweater with tiny white cats crocheted into the fabric. "This sweater has a crazy cat lady as its main character."

We spent a good half hour making up stories about

items we found. A couch that we supposed had been in the living room of a small-time madam. A pair of cork-heeled wedge shoes that, according to us, had belonged to a girl who ran off to Hollywood to make the big time and returned, penniless and heartbroken, the shoes her only reminder of how close she had come to being Someone. A pair of football pants that we guessed were discovered in a dark closet of a nursing home.

Finally, we found ourselves in the back corner, where we stumbled across a box full of men's hats.

"Ooh," I said, scooping out a Gatsby hat and setting it on my head. "This hat belonged to a rich old man who liked to golf."

"Boring," Mack said. He took the hat off my head.

I grabbed it and put it back on. "Fine. He also liked to murder people by bashing their heads in with a nine iron. And then hide their bodies in shallow graves under the sand traps."

"Better." Mack dug through the box. The hats tumbled around his hand. I saw a beige-and-black-houndstooth fedora with a red feather glued in the band and snatched it.

"Perfect," I said, reshaping the crown with my fingers. I smushed it over Mack's curls, then stood back and stared at it appraisingly. "Now, this one's a mystery." I tapped my chin. "Oh, yes, this hat belonged to a big, scruffy guy... kind of grumpy... definitely way too quiet... raging sweet tooth... but who loved a good manicure in tulip pink."

"Ha ha ha," Mack deadpanned, pulling the hat off his head.

"You should leave it. It's totally you."

"Uh-huh, whatever you say," he said, dropping it back into the box.

"No, really, it looked good on you." I retrieved the hat and headed for the cash register, where I paid a dollar for it, then turned and plunked it on his head. "You can pay me back in Skittles."

We left the store, Mack wearing his new fedora. We'd stayed inside longer than I'd realized, and it was starting to get dark outside.

"I live right down this street. My mom will give you a ride home," I said as we emerged from the trail onto the sidewalk again.

"That's okay. I'll walk," he answered.

"She won't mind. It's a long walk. And it's getting late."

"Nah, it's no problem," he said. "See you tomorrow." But before I could argue further, he'd unraveled his earbuds and was tucking them into his ears, cocking his hat back on his head as he ambled away.

Message 248
God, arrogant much? Who takes pictures of
themselves naked and sends them around?
You are not all that.

Message 249
Disgusting freak!

Vonnie caught me in the hall on the way to second period.

"Where were you? I waited in your driveway for like fifteen minutes."

"I'm sorry, I went running and I got back late. My mom gave me a ride on her way to work."

Vonnie rolled her eyes. "Seriously? Nice of you to let me know. I was tardy to first period."

"Sorry, Von, I've kind of got a lot of other things on my mind right now."

I stopped at my locker, ignoring the paper that someone had taped there. It was a Booty Call Sign-Up sheet. People had signed it with ridiculous fake names like Hung Johnson and Starr Porno. I crumpled it up and dropped it on the floor.

"Look, I get it that you're all upset right now," Vonnie said, "but you're being kind of self-centered. This is not the end of the world."

"Did you even bother to read my text?" I shot back. "My dad got a phone call from Adams yesterday. Some parents complaining about a cell phone scandal? What do you think that's about?"

"Yes, I saw it. I thought you'd want to know about the website everyone's talking about is all. I figured we could discuss the thing with your dad on the way to school today. It's not like you're really into text conversations these days. Or regular conversations, for that matter."

I gaped at her. "Do you not even care? My *dad*, Von. My dad is going to know about the text. He's probably going to see it. What if your dad saw a naked picture of you? Would it make you self-centered to care?" I shut my locker and we began walking toward class.

"Please, my dad would have to pay attention to something I was doing for five seconds, and that would never happen, so it's a moot point. Listen, the fact is you got burned by your boyfriend, things got a little out of hand, but your bod looks great and it's time to get over it."

As if on cue, a group of sophomores walked past us. One of them bumped me from behind on her way by. "Move it, ho," the sophomore shot over her shoulder as I struggled to hang on to my books. I gave Vonnie a pointed I-told-you-so look.

"The bigger deal you make out of it, the bigger deal it's going to be," she said.

"Really? Because I haven't made any deal out of it and my picture is on a website right now."

We'd reached Vonnie's art class. She stopped in the doorway and faced me. I could see a couple of girls whispering behind her at their desks. It didn't take a genius to know what they were whispering about. "Look, I get it," she said. "I'm just saying next time you decide to ditch me and get a ride with someone else, maybe you should let me know, okay?"

And the way she said it was so snotty, all I felt was rage. I might have taken the photo and sent it to Kaleb, but she was the one who'd trashed his house and car. She hadn't ever owned up to her part in this at all.

"And maybe next time you decide to go all vigilante justice and ruin my life, maybe you should let me know," I said. "Okay?"

She looked incredulous, her perfect blond eyebrows shooting up under her sideswept bangs. "Unbelievable. So now this is my fault?"

"No, it's always been your fault."

"You blame Rachel, you blame me. Dude, he's your ex-boyfriend, not ours."

"Exactly!" I said. "So you had no business butting in with your immature shaving cream pranks. Seriously, who does that anymore? What, are we still in junior high?"

The bell rang and the last few stragglers in the hallway sprinted toward their classrooms. Vonnie backed in through her classroom doorway, her arms crossed over her books, making her look tiny and taut and furious.

"Fine. You want to be on your own? You're on your own, Buttercup."

I sighed. I didn't want to be alone. Vonnie might have started the whole thing, but she wasn't the only guilty party in this mess, and she was still my best friend and I needed her. "Von..."

But she'd turned her back and was heading toward her table. My heart sank.

Finally, I headed for my class, but as I approached the door, Principal Adams stepped out of nowhere and put his hand on my elbow.

"Ashleigh, I need you to come down to the office with me."

Without the slightest pause, he turned and headed toward the administration office, and I followed, my stomach sloshing and my eyes burning, and feeling more alone than I ever had before.

I'd been in Principal Adams's office countless times.

Turning in fundraiser money, showing off a cross-country trophy, eating lunch with the people who'd made the honor roll. I'd always wondered what it would be like to be there because of trouble. I'd thought the kids who ended up in the principal's office were the losers who couldn't control themselves.

And now here I was. One of them.

It was sunny outside, and still hot, so the shades were drawn over the massive window behind Principal Adams's desk, giving the whole office a murky gray tone. The walls were lined with shelves, books bearing titles such as *Fundamentals of Teaching* and *Educating the Special Needs Child* crammed onto them. I wondered if he'd read them all. It was hard to imagine Principal Adams as an academic, given that most of his time was spent standing in the hallways nagging at people to get to their classes before the bell rang.

He gestured for me to sit down in the chair across from his desk, and after I sat, he walked out of the office, mumbled a few things to the secretary, then disappeared around the corner. I spent the time wringing my hands and swallowing repeatedly, wishing the lump in my throat would go away.

Eventually he came back with Mrs. Westlie, our school psychologist, who carried a legal pad in one hand and gave me one of those half-smiles that people give when they either don't want to talk to you or feel sorry for you. I guessed maybe it was a little of both.

They took their time getting settled, or maybe it only felt that way to me. It was so quiet in the office I swore I could hear the sweat seeping out on my forehead. Finally, Principal Adams sat behind his desk and Mrs. Westlie settled on the chair next to me, laying her legal pad on her knees and holding her pen loosely in her hand.

Principal Adams cleared his throat. "Ashleigh, how are things going for you?" he started, and I thought it was such a weird question, I was almost too surprised to answer it.

"Fine," I said, my voice weak and tiny.

"Are you sure?" Mrs. Westlie asked. I noticed her pen poised to write. She had adopted a concerned, sympathetic head-tilt to go with the patronizing smile.

I nodded.

"Well, I'll tell you why I'm asking," Principal Adams said. "Yesterday I got a phone call from a parent about a text her son had received. This morning I got three more phone calls about the same text."

I looked down at my lap, my face burning so hard I almost felt drunk. Like I was watching this happen to someone else, not me. This was on TV. It had to be. I was an observer. Only an observer. I said nothing.

"Do you know anything about this text?" Principal Adams asked, and when I still couldn't bring myself to look up, much less answer him, he continued. "Ashleigh, the text includes a photo."

I closed my eyes. Nothing worked to keep the embarrassment away. Being blind. Being deaf. Being frozen. Being an observer. Being silent. I still felt humiliated no matter what I was.

"Ashleigh," Mrs. Westlie said, her voice soft, but with an undertone of authority and seriousness, "it's clear that it's you in the photo. And even if it wasn't, your name and phone number are attached to it."

I felt a tear slither out from under my eyelid, and felt all the more disgraced for it. As much crying and dry-heaving as I'd done at home, I didn't want to cry in front of anyone at school. This was embarrassing enough without my adding to it by bawling. I made no move to wipe the tear away; maybe if I ignored it, they wouldn't see it, and it would be like it wasn't happening at all. But I felt my chin begin to crumple and my breath begin to hitch, too, and there was no way I was going to be able to keep it in any longer. Everything from the past week was going to come out—the sadness of breaking up with Kaleb, the betrayal, the embarrassment, the anger at Vonnie, all of it.

"I didn't mean for everyone to see it," I said, my voice an unsteady warble. "Kaleb sent it."

Mrs. Westlie started writing on her legal pad. "Kaleb who?" she asked without looking up.

"Coats," I said, and I had to wipe my nose with the back of my hand, which only made me cry all the harder. Principal Adams pushed a box of tissues across the desk and I took one.

"Coats?" he said. "He's graduated, hasn't he?"

I nodded. "We broke up."

Principal Adams got a deep furrow between his eyebrows when I said that. "He's eighteen, I take it?"

I nodded. I didn't understand how Kaleb mattered at all, given that he no longer went to Chesterton High, but it must have mattered to them, because Principal Adams and Mrs. Westlie exchanged a look.

"Ashleigh, how did he get this photo of you in the first place?" she asked, and I was sure my lips wouldn't move around the words, I was so humiliated. I took a deep breath to abate the tears.

"I took it," I said. "I sent it to him."

"Do you know who else has the text?" she asked.

Again I shook my head. "A lot of people," I said, and Principal Adams got a pained expression on his face.

He straightened up in his chair. "The parents who called me all have freshman students," he said. "And this morning Mrs. Martinez said she had to confiscate the phones of three sophomores. She said they were passing around a text of a naked student. Some other teachers have complained about increased cell phone use in their classrooms as well. Do you realize, Ashleigh, how disruptive this text has been? And these parents aren't going to go away. They want suspension."

I sat up straighter, alarmed. Parents had seen the photo. Teachers had seen it. Suspension. My dad would kill me. My mom would be so disappointed. She'd want to know what had happened. They both would. "Please don't tell my parents," I begged, and the tears started anew, because I couldn't believe I was at the point of begging the principal to keep a secret this big from my parents. "Please. I'll do Saturday school or something, but if you tell my parents… My dad is the superintendent."

"I know exactly who your dad is, Ashleigh, and I'm sorry, but it's too late. I've already talked to him about this problem we're having, and he asked me to forward the text. I had to warn him about what he was going to see. He already knows about your involvement."

At that moment, I could have sworn that the floor dropped about a thousand feet, my chair sailing down into a black hole. Things began to get grainy, and I must have swooned or something, because Mrs. Westlie reached over and put her hand on my shoulder.

"Are you feeling ill?" she asked.

I doubled over in my chair. My dad had seen the text. I wanted to die right then and there.

"Ashleigh," she said, shaking me a little. "Do you need to lie down in the nurse's office for a minute?"

I shook my head. I must have, because I saw the room sweep back and forth in front of my eyes, and my stomach was sinking, sinking, sinking, giving me a strange sense of vertigo.

They talked to each other for a few minutes, and I could make out enough through my daze to understand that they were talking about the logistics of my suspension. They were making decisions about what to do with this "situation" that I had caused. But in my head all I heard was a buzzing, droning noise that must have been the numbness reaching my brain, and it sounded like a horde of cicadas calling out what a horrible person I was: *Slut up for grabs! Slut up for grabs! Slut up for grabs!*

Finally, Principal Adams turned to me and said, "Right now we're going to put you on an indefinite suspension, just until we get a hold on this situation. We're going to get to the bottom of how this photo got passed around, too. Do you have any idea who might have sent it, other than your boyfriend?"

"He's my ex-boyfriend," I said through cold and dry lips. "And Nate. Nate Chisolm sent it, too, I'm pretty sure."

"The sophomore?"

"Yes. He played baseball with Kaleb."

And again they shared a look. Mrs. Westlie closed her eyes and shook her head pityingly.

Principal Adams stood up. "Mrs. Westlie will take you to your locker to get your things. We've called your dad to come get you."

Tears started up again as I stood and followed her down the hall to my locker. I pulled out my jacket and a couple of books and pushed everything else inside. I hated not knowing how long I'd be gone, how behind I'd be when I got back. If I got back. Would it be possible that I'd be gone for the rest of the year? That I'd have to switch schools? Retake my junior year?

"I need to get my cross-country things," I said, and Mrs. Westlie walked me down to the field house, then stayed outside the locker room while I went in. I pulled my gym bag out and stuffed all of my laundry, and my extra pair of running shoes, into it.

Coach Igo was in her office when I passed by to leave.

"I understand you won't be participating in this week's meet," she called out. I stopped, stepped inside. The glare of the locker room lights hurt my irritated eyes, made them feel puffy.

"No, I guess not."

"You have your lock?"

"I left it on my locker. I'm taking everything home to wash while I'm"—I couldn't make myself say it, couldn't say *suspended*—"gone."

She looked back down to the book she was notating. "Go get it," she said.

"Coach?"

She looked up. "Go get your lock and bring it to me." I stood there trying to make sense of what she was saying. "Playing a sport is a privilege, not a right. You lost that privilege. You're off the team."

For a moment, this seemed so surreal, there was no possible way it was actually happening to me. Surely I hadn't been suspended indefinitely and kicked off the cross-country team all in the space of ten minutes. It wasn't possible.

Coach stood up, her chair making an awful metallic screeching sound on the floor, and checked her watch. "Hurry, I've got a class starting in ten minutes."

I marched back through the locker room and dialed the

combination on the lock I'd been given by the school my freshman year, when I first made the team. I pulled it off, for the last time, and handed it to Coach. She gave me a semisympathetic look.

"I've known you for a while now, Ashleigh, and something tells me this whole thing was an accident or somehow got out of your control."

I nodded.

"But that doesn't change the fact that you made the poor decision that set it all in motion."

"I know." Boy, did I ever know. And know and know and know.

"And you know the rules of play. If your grades drop or you get into any trouble in the classroom, you're off the team. No exceptions. I have to do it."

She bounced the lock in her palm a few times, and if I hadn't known better, I would have thought she almost felt kind of bad about kicking me off the team.

Mrs. Westlie appeared, the clack of her heels echoing off the lockers. She poked her head around the corner. "Ashleigh? You ready? Your dad is here. He's in the office waiting for you."

Hell no, I wasn't ready. I would never be ready to face him. I still had no idea how I would do it. But I knew I couldn't stand here in the girls' locker room forever, hoping he'd go away. Eventually he'd come in here and find me. And then he'd be super-pissed—like he wasn't super-pissed already.

"I'm sorry, Coach," I said.

"I'm sorry, too, Ashleigh. You're a good runner." She shook her head sadly, which only made me feel worse.

I followed Mrs. Westlie out of the locker room. There were several boys in the gym, bouncing basketballs, and some of them stopped and watched me as I walked out. Somehow this was worse than the name-calling—the silent, curious stares. I knew what they were thinking now—they were glad it wasn't them being escorted out of the school, and they couldn't wait to gossip to their friends that they'd seen it happen to me.

Dad didn't say anything to me on the way home. We sat in complete and utter silence, which was somehow worse than if he'd been lecturing me. What had started out as a way to get Kaleb's attention now loomed between us in the front seat of Dad's car, big and ugly and dense.

When we got home, Dad got out of the car and disappeared into the house, leaving me behind. I sat in silence for a few minutes, listening to the ticking and clicking of the engine cooling off, then gathered my things and went inside, racing straight to my room and locking the door. I half-expected Dad to come storming in at any moment, ready to rage at me, but he never did. I sat on my bed, miserably deleting texts and watching the sun get lower in the sky as the afternoon wore on.

My phone rang. It was Vonnie. I could hear the squeak of shoes on the gym floor as her teammates warmed up. "I told Coach I have cramps, so she's letting me take five," she whispered into the phone. "But I heard you got suspended so I wanted to make sure you're okay."

"I guess."

"Did your dad freak out?"

"Not yet," I said. "He's going to kill me."

I heard a whistle, and Vonnie's voice went lower. "He'll get over it. It's not like you're the first person to ever get in trouble. He'll be mad, probably yell at you for a while, and then he'll forget about it."

"I doubt that," I said, then paused. "I'm sorry. About the fight. I was acting like a jerk."

"No big. I mean, I don't love that you think this was all my fault, but it's okay. You're stressed. I get it."

"I don't think it's all your fault, Von."

"I probably didn't help things with the shaving cream," she said.

"Probably not," I agreed. "By the way, I got kicked off cross-country, too."

"Nuh-uh!"

"Yep. My life is basically over. I have nothing. No Kaleb—not that I want him, anyway—no school, no cross-country. I'll be grounded for life, I'm sure. I don't even have my dignity anymore."

"I'm sorry, Buttercup." She paused. "But you've got great boobs. Everyone knows that." She chuckled, her breath making a whoosh into the phone, and when I didn't laugh, she asked, "Too soon?"

"Maybe a little." But I smiled in spite of myself. Somehow joking about it made it feel the tiniest bit like it was not the end of the world.

There was some muffled talking in the background and Vonnie's voice, also muffled as if she was covering the phone with her hand, answered. "I know something that might make you feel better. Or worse. I don't know. And then I've gotta go."

"What?"

"Some other people got suspended today, too."

"Who?"

"Nate Chisolm," she said. "And that Silas kid, because they were the ones who started the whole thing. They're saying Kaleb sent it to Nate and told him to have fun and do whatever he wanted with it. They're in big trouble."

"Good," I said.

Vonnie paused. "And Rachel."

"Rachel who?"

"Wellby."

I couldn't believe my ears. Rachel, the one who was so offended that I'd said she was partially to blame for talking me into taking the picture? Rachel, the one who thought it was no big deal because her brother's slutty freshman girlfriend did it all the time? Rachel, the one who was so traumatized by being asked if we were lovers?

"What for?"

"You sure you want to know?"

"I don't know—do I?"

"Probably not." Vonnie paused again and I could hear the slam of a bathroom stall door. "She's the one who attached your name and phone number to the text."

"What? Are you kidding me?"

"I wish I was. And don't be mad at me...but I kinda guessed it was her all along, because she sent it to me when she did it. She's such a twit to think I wouldn't mind. But she says she wasn't trying to be mean or anything. It was supposed to be a joke."

"You knew? When we were talking about it at lunch, you knew and didn't say anything?"

"I know. I'm a horrible friend. If it makes you feel any better, I didn't know for sure then. But someone turned her in to Principal Adams. She's in deep shit."

I was so angry, I didn't have any words. My lips were pressed tightly together and my ears felt hot. Quickly, her voice echoing off the locker room walls, Vonnie filled me in on all the details about how, during sixth period, Principal Adams got on the intercom and told the teachers to confiscate any cell phones that were out, and how Mrs. Blankenship took like half the class's cell phones. And how people were seriously pissed and were threatening that their parents were going to call and complain about it, because they paid for those cell phones and they weren't the school's property to take.

"Oh, and a woman was hanging around the front doors of the school talking to Principal Adams after school let out, and people were saying she's a reporter," Vonnie finished.

My mind whirled. I tried to take it all in, but it was too much. On one hand, it felt good to not be the only one in trouble anymore. But on the other hand, I was still humiliated and would still have to face my parents. I would still have to face everyone at school again eventually. I would still have to face Rachel, and would Vonnie expect me to play nice with her? Probably. *She says she wasn't trying to be mean or anything*, Vonnie had been quick to point out, which sounded to me like she was defending her friend. But who would defend me? Vonnie? The longer this went on, the less likely that looked. And even if she did, if you're the kind of person who defends everyone, does your defense really mean anything?

Vonnie went back to practice and I hung up, flopping on my bed and staring at the ceiling, my phone clutched to my chest. If there ever was a situation that had gotten out of control, this was it. People were going down fast, and I wondered how much worse it would get before it got any better.

Finally, my mom called for me. I was about to find out how much worse it would get in my house, anyway.

They hadn't turned on the lights yet, and it was getting close to evening outside, making the whole den shadowy and frightening. At least in a darkened room I wouldn't have to face the humiliation of meeting their eyes.

I walked in and sat down in the chair closest to the door without them even asking.

"You are in so much trouble," my dad started, and the tone of his voice was downright scary. I didn't think I had ever heard his voice sound so slithery in my entire life. I didn't answer him. I felt like silence was the right move.

"Ashleigh, what on earth?" my mom chimed in, and her voice sounded much closer to tears. For some reason, that scared me even more.

"I'm sorry, Mom," I said.

"Sorry?" Dad boomed. "You're sorry? You think saying you're sorry is going to fix this? This is no minor thing, Ashleigh. This is going to stick to you like glue for a long, long time. Did you know a reporter came to the school today? She already knew that you were my daughter. Someone had told her. For God's sake, Ashleigh, are you trying to ruin me?"

"No, Dad, I didn't ever mean for any of this to happen." Even though I tried to stay silent, and even though I didn't think there were any more tears left, words and tears spilled out of me. I knew it would only enrage him more, but I couldn't help myself.

"I've got this pain-in-the-ass board president up in my face all the time," he was saying, "and as if that's not enough, now I've got a sexting scandal in my school district."

Mom made a whimpering noise at the word "sexting."

"And as if *that* isn't enough, the person whose naked

picture is causing parents to breathe fire down my neck is my own daughter!"

The last three words boomed out of his mouth so loudly I thought I heard pictures rattle against the walls around me. I winced.

"Well, if it makes you feel any better, my life sucks right now, too, Dad. Everyone is making fun of me and calling me names. This has been the worst day of my life, do you even care?"

"You brought that on yourself!" he shouted. "So I have little sympathy."

"Roy, calm down. Shouting at her isn't going to make anything better," Mom said in that same weird, wavery voice.

"I know that. You know how I know that? Because nothing...*nothing* is going to make this better," he said. "I've already gotten a dozen phone calls today, wanting to know what I'm going to do about this. And I can't tell them, because all I can think about is that photograph that I will never be able to get out of my head, Ashleigh. I will never be able to unsee it. Thank you for that." He paced in the small space between Mom's desk and the doorway.

"I'm sorry, Dad. It was a stupid mistake. What more do you want me to say? I only meant for Kaleb to see it."

"Don't say his name," Dad said, his teeth clenched. "Don't even say that little son of a bitch's name."

"Were you two having sex?" Mom interjected.

"No, I swear, we never did."

"Of course they were," Dad answered. "You can't believe her, Dana, after what she's done."

"Give her a chance," Mom said. "She's never lied to us before."

"That we know of."

"I'm not lying," I said.

But Dad wasn't having any of it. He was so angry, all he could do was yell and seethe. "I don't care. I don't care about that right now. I care about what's going to happen next. What do you think I should do, Ashleigh? I'd love to hear your thoughts, since this is your mess."

"What do you mean? I got suspended."

"That's not going to be enough. These people are really angry. We've got a major problem on our hands, and I don't think you understand how major. There's going to have to be more. They're going to call for more. Publicly. That reporter isn't going away."

More? How was suspending me and three other people not enough? How was kicking me off the cross-country team and taking me away from my friends and from school not enough? I hadn't killed anybody. I hadn't even hurt anybody. I'd made a stupid mistake and it had gotten out of hand, and I was already so mortified. How could people want more? And what kind of more would they want, anyway?

"I don't know," I said. "I don't know what you mean by more."

"Well, for one thing, we'll start by taking your cell

phone," Mom added, and the shadows had gotten so deep at this point, I really couldn't even see her face back there behind her computer monitor. "Clearly, you can't use texts appropriately."

"We broke up," I argued. "It's not like I'm going to be sending him any more texts. Especially not that kind."

"You shouldn't ever have been sending that kind in the first place. We thought you knew that already, but apparently we should have been monitoring you like a four-year-old," Dad said, and then he, thankfully, stormed out. I heard the cabinets opening and closing in the kitchen, and ice cubes dropping into a glass.

The room felt empty without him there. No, more than empty. It felt sucked out. Devoid of oxygen. With him gone, so was my defensiveness. Now I was left with just Mom, and embarrassment and sorrow.

"You got kicked off the team," she said.

"I know," I answered. "I don't really think that's fair. This had nothing to do with cross-country."

"Fair isn't for you to decide now," she said. "You lost that privilege."

"Mom, it wasn't my fault that it got sent around. That was Nate's and Silas's and Rachel's fault. And Kaleb's. He shouldn't ever have sent it to anyone."

"But they wouldn't have had anything to send if you hadn't taken the photo in the first place," she said, but she didn't sound argumentative so much as scared. Which scared me.

"What's going to happen?" I asked.

"I don't know," she answered. "But it starts with your phone." I saw movement in the shadows, and could barely make out her hand, stretching across the desk toward me, looking pale and fragile in the evening light. I pulled my phone out of my pocket and turned it off, then placed it in her hand. "And I would say that you're grounded. For a long time," she said. "We'll go with indefinitely on that, too."

I'd figured as much.

The TV blared to life in the living room, and I heard the squeak of the recliner's footrest snapping into place. Mom didn't say any more, and Dad was clearly done with me. All I wanted to do was go to my room.

I got up to leave but turned back. "Mom, please don't be disappointed in me."

"How could I not be?" she asked in that same tired, wet voice.

I guessed I couldn't blame her for that. How could she not be?

"What more do you think Dad means?" I asked.

"I don't know," she answered, and that was what worried me most of all.

I climbed the stairs to my room, where I didn't turn on the light all night. Just stayed in the dark, wrapped around myself, waiting for more to happen.

Whatever horrible thing "more" was.

SEPTEMBER

Message Inbox Full

The next day I slept in. On the one hand, this was a good thing, because it meant I didn't have to see Mom or Dad before they left for work. On the other hand, it meant I woke up to a quiet house.

I had no cell phone, so I couldn't text Vonnie to see what was happening at school. I still had my laptop, but everyone else was in class, so there was nobody to talk to.

All I had was the TV—which sucked during the day—and my running shoes.

Even though I was grounded, exercise didn't really count as "going out," did it? Especially not to my mom, who was so upset that I'd been kicked off the team. Maybe seeing that I was willing to keep working at it would make her a little less mad at me.

I ate lunch and then got into my running gear. I stuffed a few dollars into my shoe and took off.

But once I got outside, I felt like everyone was looking at me. Staring at the naked girl whose picture had ended up on their kids' cell phones.

I knew it wasn't the truth—probably nobody was looking at me—but the very thought still made me feel nervous.

I hit the trail and raced through the woods faster than usual, trying to pound out all the emotions I was feeling with my footsteps.

Finally, I ended up at the thrift store, which was open, though the parking lot was empty save for one car. I went inside, my shirt soaked with sweat, my breathing still coming in gasps.

"Hello," a white-haired woman in a fuzzy sweater said as I came inside. Who wore a sweater in heat like this? I stood in front of a fan she had going next to the register.

"Hi."

"Purple tags are twenty percent off today," she said. "Are you looking for something in particular?"

Anonymity. Freedom. Peace. Do you sell any of those here? Are those purple-tag items? Because I would think they'd be full price if anything was. Hot commodities.

I shook my head. "Just looking."

She went back to attaching price tags to things, and I ducked into the racks of clothes and shoes, idly digging through old skirts and blazers from the 1990s and sneakers with curled-up toes.

I passed the board games and old television sets and voice recorders. They all seemed ugly and dusty and out of style. They made the past seem depressing, and I was at once thrilled that I had not been a part of the time when those things were the best we could do and sad with the knowledge that all too soon our technology would seem as old and outdated as theirs.

I turned the corner into housewares and rambled around in there for a while. Old china teacups and saucers lined the shelves. Chipped, ugly, mismatched. Someone would buy them. Someone would find a use for a single pea-green teacup. There was a ceramic creamer with a cow wearing a bikini lounging across the lid. A fondue set with no skewers. A whole stack of dog food dishes painted with cartoon paw prints. And a bin of pillows, the top one of which had a photo of three muddy kids mugging for the camera silk-screened onto the top of it, along with the saying A PICTURE'S WORTH A THOUSAND WORDS needlepointed in fancy script. I picked it up and studied it. Why would someone get rid of this? Why would someone all of a sudden not want a photo of these children anymore?

Clutching the pillow, I turned in a slow circle and took in all the clothes and toys and shoes and dishes and furniture around me. None of it was wanted anymore. Most of it was probably forgotten. How sad.

Yet something about that realization also heartened me.

As frustrated as I was with Vonnie and her "it'll all blow over" attitude, and as much as it didn't feel like it would *ever* blow over, maybe it really would. Maybe this would eventually be forgotten, this trouble I was in. Maybe people would forget about it like this old VCR and the cassette tape player that I wasn't even sure if I'd know how to work.

Back when I was born, my parents didn't own a computer yet. They didn't send emails or surf the Internet, and they certainly didn't send texts, much less picture texts. How much had changed in that short period of time. This would change, too, and soon nobody would care about the dumb photo I'd sent to my boyfriend back when people were doing something so outdated as texting. The thought gave me hope. If someone didn't mind tossing out a photo of their children having fun, surely eventually my photo would end up in recycle bins, too.

So while she was wrong about how quickly people would forget, maybe Vonnie was right; eventually this, too, would pass. If only I lived through it in the meantime.

I checked the tag on the pillow. Three dollars. And it was a purple tag. I had enough.

I slipped off my shoe and pulled out the money I'd brought, then slipped it back on and made my way to the register.

"Find something?" the old lady asked, and I placed the pillow on the counter. "Oh, that's cute," she said, studying it.

The fan whirred toward me, blowing back my hair and sending a gust of cool air down the nape of my neck. I shuddered, my skin rising up in goose bumps. After being in here, it was going to feel outrageously hot outside.

She rang up my pillow and I paid her.

"Tomorrow we'll have green tags fifty percent off," she offered. "You should come back. We have some cute junior clothes that will get put out tonight."

"Thanks," I said, and had to tamp down the fear that I *would* be coming back to the thrift store tomorrow. And every day after that. That this would be my only respite, my only social life, talking about cute throw pillows to a seventy-year-old. *Surely*, I thought, *"indefinitely" doesn't mean forever. I can't be hanging out in a thrift store forever.*

I plunged back outside into the heat and started jogging the minute I hit the parking lot, the bag with my new pillow in it hanging over my wrist and smacking into my knee with every step.

Empowered by it, I turned into the woods and took the trail back to my house.

When I got home I went straight up to my room, kicking my shoes off in the doorway. I placed the pillow at the head of my bed, on top of my other pillows, then stood back and studied it. I liked it there. It gave me something to hope for.

I took a shower and got dressed, did some math that I figured we were probably doing in class that day. I read a little. Watched a movie. Poked around online until I worked up the nerve to look for the website where my photo had been posted. Someone had taken it down, along with all the nasty comments, which was good, though I wondered if that only meant my photo had been moved somewhere else.

After a while, I heard a car coming down my street,

someone pulling into my driveway, and then two short honks. Vonnie.

I ran downstairs and opened the front door to let her in.

"Oh my God, Buttercup, you wouldn't believe," she said, pushing past me and heading straight for the recliner. She plopped into it sideways. "There were like twenty parents up in the office this morning. People are pissed off."

"About what?" I sat on the arm of the couch.

She shrugged. "About the texts. About the school taking away phones. About it being the superintendent's daughter. People's parents want him fired. Sarah's mom is saying it should go to court."

"Well, that's rich, considering it was Sarah's brother who started the whole thing," I said. But on the inside I was trembling. The peace I'd felt when I'd gotten home from the thrift store was gone. I was slammed back into reality, where I'd screwed up majorly and everyone in the world knew it. "Besides, court? What for?"

She waved her hand. "I don't know. You know Sarah. It could have been all drama. You got any soda?"

I brought her a soda, and she opened it and took a sip, shaking her head. "What are you gonna do, Buttercup?"

"What do you mean? I'm suspended, remember? It's not like I can do anything."

"No, I mean...what if this gets serious? What are you gonna do if Sarah's mom gets this to go to court or whatever?"

My heart was leaping around in my chest like a wild

animal, but I swallowed it down and waved my hand dismissively. "Drama," I reminded her. "I mean, it can't go to court. It's not like I committed a crime or something."

"I guess," she said. "But I probably ought to tell you, this is totally the only thing everybody is talking about right now. It's in the newspaper and people are writing all these letters to the editor and stuff. And the text is still being sent around. I heard that some people over in Mayville have it."

Mayville High School? How many schools had this gone to? Chesterton, the junior high, two colleges, and now Mayville.

"No way. I don't even know anybody in Mayville."

She nodded, took another sip. "Probably a good thing, right? Adams is trying to figure out who's still sending it around. The shit's getting really deep. Saturday detention if you're caught talking about it, suspension if you're caught sending it. But of course nobody's going to tell if they got it sent to them. They don't want to be caught up in this."

"Neither do I," I said, and I felt my chin start to quiver again. I willed the feeling away.

We sat together for a while, and a couple times she tried to bring up another subject—somebody was dating someone new, someone had gotten into a wreck in the parking lot, somebody was fighting over something stupid—but I honestly couldn't pay attention, and she didn't even really have much conviction behind her stories. It was like my story was the only story worth telling right now, and if we couldn't talk about that, there was really no point in talking at all.

Finally, she set her empty can on the table next to the recliner, stretched, and got up. "I probably should go," she said. "You gonna be okay?"

I shrugged. "I guess it sounds like I'm going to be here for a while."

She looked sympathetic. "Buttercup. Take it from me, you don't want to be there. Have you talked to Rachel?"

"No," I said sullenly. And I had no plans to ever talk to her again.

"She says she's sorry she did it. She says it was supposed to be funny. Your face was in the picture, so she figured everybody knew it was you anyway. She wasn't thinking it would go this far."

I laughed. "Like destroy my reputation and get me suspended? Well, I don't forgive her."

Vonnie looked torn. "I get it," she finally said, but I didn't believe that getting it meant she was going to see it my way and stop hanging around with Rachel. And it was at that moment that I really understood how my relationship with Vonnie had changed.

Not long after Vonnie left, Mom came home. Her hair was kind of fuzzy, like she'd run her hands through it a lot during the day, and she looked tired.

Instead of getting out a book or heading straight to the computer in the den, she went to the bedroom and climbed into bed, slinging one arm over her eyes.

"Mom?" I asked, standing in the darkened doorway. "You fine?"

At first she didn't answer, but then I heard a muffled "No."

I went in and lay down next to her, stiff and alert next to her defeated body. "Bad day at work?"

She moved her arm and looked out at me with one eye. "Bad day in general," she said. "Your dad is going to be late tonight, and I have a migraine, so just grab yourself something for dinner."

Her tone sounded angry and bitter. And tired. Really, really tired. She sounded a lot like I felt.

"Okay. Why's Dad going to be late?"

She sighed, letting her arm fall to her side, staring up at the ceiling. "You really want to know, Ashleigh? He's having a meeting."

"About the text?"

"Of course about the text." I hated the way she sounded. Mom had been mad at me before, but she'd never sounded so much like she wanted to get away from me.

"I'm sorry, Mom," I said again, even though I'd already said it once and had really meant it. I was getting really tired of apologizing, and I'd noticed that I was the only one doing it. A lot of people were involved in this, but only one of us was saying she was sorry. And nobody was apologizing to me. "I heard there've been reporters hanging out around the school. Is that who he's meeting with?"

"Yes, he's had to talk to reporters. They've scooped up the story like vultures. I think they're forgetting that this involves children."

"You think they're going to put it on the news?" I got a lump in my throat and tried to concentrate on the afternoon shadows sliding around on the ceiling and walls of my parents' darkened bedroom, the slits of light pushing through the edges of the drawn blackout shades. "Do you think they'll come here?"

"I don't know," she said. "They're already at Central Office. Part of what makes the story so sensational is that you're the superintendent's daughter, so who knows how they'll handle it." She moaned. "But who cares what the reporters are going to do, anyway?" she said.

I sat up. "I do, Mom. This is so humiliating. I think everybody's so worried about how this looks for them, they're forgetting how embarrassing this is for me. I'm naked in that picture."

She pulled herself to sitting and faced me, the lines around her eyes soaking up the shadows of the room, making her look older and slightly witchy.

"It's embarrassing for all of us. But this is bigger than just embarrassment."

I blinked. "What do you mean?"

"Ashleigh," she answered. "This isn't going to stop at embarrassment. What you've done…you've distributed child pornography. Your dad…he's going to be late tonight because he's meeting with the police. You're going to be arrested."

We stared at each other in disbelief.

More was so much scarier than I'd ever imagined.

COMMUNITY SERVICE

I brought the pillow with me to Teens Talking.

I felt kind of stupid walking in there with a silk-screen picture of little kids peeking out of my backpack like a security blanket, but I had an idea and I wanted to run with it.

"What's this?" Darrell said, coming up behind me in the hallway and pulling the pillow out of my backpack. He studied it. "Awww, cute. Your brothers?"

I shook my head. "I'm an only child."

"Oooh, spoooiled," he sang, and stuffed the pillow back into my bag like he couldn't care less about it.

"Please, like you couldn't tell she's spoiled by looking at her," Kenzie said, brushing past me with her big belly. I rolled my eyes but let it go.

Mack was already at his computer. Instead of sitting next to him, I went straight to the back of the room, where a table was set up right next to the art cabinet. I'd already checked ahead of time, so I knew exactly what I needed and where to find it. I got to work, arranging a bunch of random items haphazardly across the table—crayons, a pencil cup, a stuffed bear, a rubber band ball, a flashlight, and my cell phone. Right in the center, tilted almost diagonally, I placed the pillow on top of all of it, then stood back and snapped a photo.

"Check it out," I said, pushing the camera's review tab as I walked past Mack's computer station. I bumped him in the back and he turned around and looked at the camera's screen. I saw his lips move as he read the words across the pillow. "For my pamphlet. What do you think?"

He nodded. "Nice."

The time flew by as I worked on editing the photo until it was perfect. I took three more shots, adjusting the items here and there to get it just right. But something about it seemed bland. I couldn't quite land on what was missing.

When Mrs. Mosely stood up and looped her purse strap over her shoulder, saying, "All right, everyone, you're two hours closer to being done with my ugly mug," followed by Darrell saying, "Aw, Mose, your mug ain't ugly. You remind me of my mom," I'd barely noticed that any time had passed.

We filed out, and I peeked into Dad's office, only to find a sticky note on the door saying he was in a late meeting and I'd need to catch a ride with Mom. But as I pulled out my cell phone to call her, I noticed Mack heading down the sidewalk, his jean jacket pulled up around his ears. I texted Mom that I'd be walking and burst through the doors after him instead.

"I'm going with you," I said, trotting up next to Mack on the sidewalk.

"Where?"

I shrugged. "Wherever you're going. Skate park?"

He considered it. "Sure, okay."

When we got to the skate park, we both ran up the closest ramp and sat down at the top as if this was something we'd done together a million times rather than only once. I shrugged out of my backpack and let it rest behind me. Mack kicked off his shoes and set them to the side. I did the same, even though my socks were thin and my toes were already cold from the walk over.

"See that rail over there?" Mack said, pointing to a nearly rusted-through rail stretched between two low ramps. "I saw a kid break his arm on that thing once. His bone was broken in half and his arm just swung around all limp." He stood and leaned forward over the ramp, then slid down on his socks.

"Gross!" I followed him.

"Yeah, it was. My dad had to take him to the hospital. But the kid was back here the next week, skating with his arm in a cast."

We jogged up the lowest ramp and slid down the other side, then sprinted toward the highest ramp and pushed ourselves up, our legs pumping as our socks slid, our fingers gripping the ledge above us. We made it to the top and stopped to catch our breath.

"And another time I saw a kid knock both his front teeth out trying to take his bike down that ramp over there."

He slid down the ramp, but I stayed put, my hands on my hips, my toes numb, my fingers red from the cold. I felt out of shape since leaving cross-country.

"What about you?" I called. "You ever get hurt here?"

As if on cue, he misstepped and tumbled down a ramp, doing a clumsy backward somersault and landing on the concrete.

"Not yet," he said, rubbing the back of his head as he sat up. "But keep talking and maybe I will."

I sat and slid down on my butt like a little kid, ending a foot or so away from him. "Sorry. You okay?"

He squinted at me and smiled. "I've wiped out worse than that lots of times. I'm just not used to having anyone out here with me to see it. Not since my dad"—he hesitated, turning away—"stopped bringing me here. It's been a while."

There was definitely something weird about the way Mack looked when he talked about his dad, but something told me to let it go. I knew enough about Mack to know that if I started asking a bunch of questions, he would clam up. So instead I lay back against the ramp with my arms crossed under my head and watched the clouds, which were slowly moving by. I heard Mack run up the ramp again, and heard him slide down. And then again. And then the last time I heard him run up, there was a pause. I glanced over to see him tying his shoes.

"Leaving already?" I asked. I knew I was hardly being the most exciting conversationalist in the world, but that usually didn't matter with Mack. I wasn't ready to leave yet. I liked it here.

"I owe you."

I sat up. He tossed my backpack and then shoes down to me, first one, then the other. It felt good to put them on. My toes were so cold. "What do you owe me?"

He jumped off the edge of the ramp, landing on his feet but stumbling forward a few steps before getting control. "The creek."

I grabbed my backpack and we plunged into the woods and turned a sharp right, walking away from the skate park. Our shoes crunched on the dead sticks and leaves that littered the ground for the winter. Despite all the trees losing their leaves, it was surprisingly secluded in there, and even though I could hear cars on a street somewhere ahead of us and could see mottled sides of houses through the dead branches and scant leaves, I couldn't help feeling cut off from civilization.

We tromped over a patch of dirt that might have at one point been a trail, and then we came upon a small creek, running dry save for a few puddles here and there.

"This is it?"

"Yep."

"There's no water," I said. "Maybe I'm wrong, but I guess I always assumed that creeks had water."

Mack simply kept walking, shimmying sideways until he was standing in the creek bed, which he followed, and then ducked into a concrete tube. "Come on." His voice echoed off the walls.

After a moment's hesitation, I followed him down into the creek and peered into the dark tunnel. I could walk in there bending only slightly at the waist, but I wasn't sure I wanted to. Places like this were teeming with bugs and rodents. "Mack!" I called, and he popped back out to the entrance.

"Come on, chickenshit," he said. "It's just a drainage pipe. It's not a sewer or anything. And it's dry." I stood there a second longer, unmoving. "Fine, suit yourself," he said, turning and going back inside. "You're the one who wanted to see it, anyway."

I took a deep breath, watching the back of his jean jacket until I couldn't see him anymore. If my parents knew I was spending my time after Teens Talking following a boy like Mack—a boy I'd met in community service and barely knew, besides—into a drainage ditch, where I could possibly be raped and murdered, they would come unglued. And who could blame them?

But I followed him in anyway.

It wasn't as bad inside the drainage pipe as I'd feared. It was dank, and there were sodden leaves underfoot, and a distant sound of dripping that echoed off the concrete walls around me, but there were no rats or spiders' nests pregnant with pulsating eggs or anything like that, and I could see the exit hole ahead in the distance.

Mack was waiting for me inside. He bent down and picked up something, then held it out to me: a flashlight.

Even though it was more shadowy than all-out dark, I flipped on the flashlight, if for no other reason than that I was still uncertain what we were doing in there.

Mack raised his arm and pointed straight ahead. "So all this does is go under Cypress Street," he said. "It comes out in the same creek on the other side. Like a little tunnel. The storm drains up on the street drain down into here, but it hasn't rained in like a month, so right now everything's pretty dry. Come on."

I followed him forward, shining the light on the ground where I was going to be walking, still not convinced that I wasn't going to step in anything gross or dangerous. We tromped through the leaves, the sound of our footfalls and our breathing bouncing off the walls around us. Every now and then there'd be a low whoosh of a car driving on the street we were walking under.

Finally, I saw a rectangle of light shining through the storm drains above us. The tunnel widened out, the rounded ceiling flattening. Mack stopped between the drains.

"When it rains, you get two waterfalls down here," he said. "I like to stand in between and just listen sometimes. But you have to scoot up the wall a little or you'll be standing in water the whole time."

I pointed the flashlight up and tried to imagine what it must be like under the street in a storm, the rain beating on the world above, pouring down on either side of you, but you standing safe against the wall, listening.

Mack backed up and leaned against the curved wall.

"You come down here a lot?" I asked.

"Not as much as I used to. It's a good place to think. A good place to get away. It's hidden. I like solitude. "

I flicked off the flashlight and backed up next to him.

"You let me hang around," I said.

"I didn't know I had a choice," he answered, and then he chuckled.

I thought about all the times I'd sat next to him. The times I'd barged into his spot by the vending machines. Sat by him on the bench outside Central Office. Jogged up next to him on the sidewalk. Demanded to listen to his music. Demanded to go with him.

"No, I guess you didn't," I said.

We were silent for a minute, and I began pulling leaves off the floor and crumbling them between my fingers.

"I'll show you something. Turn your light on," he said, and I did. "Shine it on that wall over there."

I aimed the beam at the wall directly across from us and gasped. How had I not noticed before? It was covered from top to bottom with graffiti, some scratched into the stone, some written in bold, black letters, most spray-painted in vivid colors. Words, art, messages, names. I stood and

228

walked to the wall, then reached out my hand and brushed my fingers across it. "Did you do this?"

"Some. A lot of people add to it. Here, give me the flashlight."

I handed it over and he shined the light on a spot above my head. The words ROGER S 6-22-70 were scratched into the concrete, white faded to gray.

"I think that's where it started," he said. "I can't find anything older." He moved the beam. "This one's my favorite." I shuffled to the side to take a look. In bright-green cartoonish letters was the word RHINO, the "O" embellished with a horn. Next to it, in pink spray paint, was CLEVER WUZZ HERE, and beneath that were the words PEACE DRIVER.

"So cool," I said, studying every word and illustration as Mack took a step back to let the flashlight illuminate a bigger section of the wall. "Where's yours?"

He stepped forward again and bent to shine the light closer to the ground. "Here's one," he said. I squatted next to him and looked. In black lettering, the word SOLO was written. Above it were a shaded moon and a shaft of moonlight shining down on the word.

"Is that your nickname?" I asked. "Solo?"

"No, my nickname is Mack."

"Short for...?"

He sighed. "My real name is Henry. My dad started calling me Mack when I was a little kid because I've always been big like a truck. It stuck."

"So what does Solo mean?" I asked, but he didn't answer.

Instead, he stood up and pointed the light at another spot. "My dad put this one here when I was a kid."

It was very simple, very plain, almost as plain as Roger's initial inscription. DRAGON AND MACK MAY 1998.

I ran my fingers across the word DRAGON. There were so many questions I wanted to ask. So many things I wanted to find out. But Mack never offered information. He liked his solitude. And it was one thing to make him let me come with him to the skate park or the creek; to demand he take me along to his past felt like stealing.

"You want to tag it?" he asked.

"Me?"

"Yeah, why not? I've got a marker."

"What would I write?"

"I don't know. Your name. Whatever you want. You have any nicknames?"

I stared at the wall. Yes, I had a nickname. My whole life was about nicknames right now.

"Sure, give me your marker," I said, my throat suddenly burning. "I'll just write Slut Up for Grabs. Everybody'll know who left that one. But I could shorten it to Slut or Whore if we're wanting to conserve space."

"That's not what I meant. I meant, like—"

"No, I know what you meant," I said. "But if I wrote Ash or Buttercup or some other stupid nickname, what would it really mean? That's not who I am anymore. All

I am is the Slut Up for Grabs. That's all anyone cares about."

"You're not those things." Mack's voice was soft, and he'd clicked off his flashlight.

"How do you know who I am? Even I'm not sure anymore. I did it, you know? I took the picture. So if taking that picture makes me a slut, then how can I deny that I'm a slut?"

And I realized how much I'd come to believe that. Taking the picture was a mistake, but somehow that mistake had started to become me. How could I keep fighting it, keep denying the truth? It was hard to stand up for yourself—to claim that you weren't the slut they were all saying you were—when your picture was on a porn site. How could I blame them, really, for making assumptions about me? How could I blame the people on the website and at school for harassing me? How could I blame Mom and Dad for assuming I was having sex with Kaleb?

"That's ridiculous, Ashleigh. Those people don't get to say who you are. You can't let them have that kind of power. You made a mistake. You're human."

"But don't you see?" I said, my voice going croaky and loud in the enclosed space. "They do have that power. Because when I think about who I am, all I can think about is that picture."

"Then you need to think harder," he said.

I shook my head. "Forget I said anything. I...don't want to write my name up there right now is all."

"Okay," he said. "No big deal."

I tried to lean against the concrete again, hoping for the same thrill of adventure and the excitement of seclusion I'd felt before he'd shown me the graffiti.

But the walls had begun to close in on me, and the darkness had begun to press into my eyes, making me feel terrified and small. I had to get out of there.

"Thanks for bringing me, but I need to get home. See you tomorrow," I croaked, and even though I was pretty sure I felt his hand brush against my elbow, I turned and raced out the way we had come. I plunged through the woods, past the skate park, and ran all the way home, without so much as looking back once.

COMMUNITY SERVICE

At restroom break the next day, I didn't follow Mack out to the vending machines. I was embarrassed to talk to him. I felt like I needed to apologize, but I wasn't sure for what. For making him show me his most secret space and then rushing out on him? For losing it when he asked about my nickname? For forcing my friendship on him in the first place?

When he returned after the break, he dropped a roll of Life Savers on my desk. We didn't make eye contact or say a word. After a while, I picked it up and peeled it open. Earlier in the day, Phillip Moses had called me a slut, and two sophomores had giggled and whispered the entire time I was in the bathroom with them. A guy in my third-period class had acted like he was grabbing my boobs for half an hour.

But Angela Firestone had actually talked to me in PE, and at lunch some girls sat a few seats down from me like it was no big deal. Even Cheyenne kind of shyly grinned at me in the hallway as we walked past each other, when normally she would have pretended I didn't exist at all. And the fact that I had noticed those little details made me wonder if I wasn't doing what Mack had suggested in the tunnel the night before. *Then you need to think harder*, he'd said. Maybe things were just getting better on their own. Or maybe I was thinking harder.

Dad had another late night ahead of him, so Mom drove me home from community service. I took my backpack and headed straight to my room. I was only there a few minutes before I heard a light knock on my door and Vonnie came in.

"Hey," she said, kind of awkwardly waving.

I sat on my bed and stared at her because I didn't know what else to do. I'd all but given up on Vonnie, which wasn't easy. When I'd gotten back from suspension, she seemed to have moved on. There was no space for me in her life anymore, and most of the time she walked right past me as if she didn't even know who I was.

What was more, I'd found that Rachel had been eating at my old lunch table. And since we were court ordered to have nothing to do with each other, I had to stay away, which meant, essentially, that Vonnie had chosen Rachel over me.

How did you go ahead and accept that your best friend who you'd loved forever had ditched you when something that happened to you made her look bad?

"Hey," I said, suspiciously. "What's up?"

She fiddled with the end of the knitted pink scarf that was dangling loosely around her neck. She was also wearing a new pair of boots. They were white suede with rhinestones covering the toes and heels and were totally beautiful. I'd noticed them at school a few days ago and had almost run up to her to tell her how great they looked, but then I'd remembered that there was this huge hole between us now and I couldn't approach her—not even to tell her that I loved her boots—or I'd fall in.

"I just missed you," she said. "We haven't talked in forever. You okay?"

I'd freaked out in a drainage ditch last night and run away from the one person in the world who still believed in me. I was avoiding my dad, who came home late and sulked and drank every night. I'd watched my ex-boyfriend cry during an apology and I still didn't feel sorry for him. Were those things okay? I didn't know what okay looked like anymore. It had been so long since I'd seen it. But Vonnie didn't need to know any of that, especially since I still wasn't sure if I could even trust why she was standing in my bedroom. "I guess," I said. "I don't have a ton of friends these days, but I'll survive."

She lowered herself to the carpet and sat cross-legged, the way she always did when she came over, as if nothing had ever changed between us.

"I'm sorry, Buttercup," she said. "I know I've been a really rotten best friend."

"Yeah," I said. She had, and I didn't see any reason to pretend that she hadn't. Granted, I'd never been in her position before, but I could almost guarantee that I would've stuck by her. I wouldn't have run away to save my own reputation.

Or at least I liked to think I wouldn't have. But would I? Because there was a time in my life when I'd have said I would never take a naked photo of myself and send it to someone.

She fiddled with the rhinestones on her boot. "You think you can forgive me? I'm really sorry. I miss you."

"You still hanging out with Rachel?" I asked.

"Not much."

"Because she's a bitch, Vonnie, and you're going to have to choose between us." I hadn't really thought this over much. The words had popped out of my mouth without my meaning them to. But I was okay with it, because it was the truth. If Vonnie was going to be Rachel's friend, then she couldn't be mine. Like Mack had said, I deserved a better best friend than that.

"Then I choose you. Totally," she said, without even pausing to think about it.

I felt like maybe I shouldn't forgive her. Like I should put it off—make her sweat it out or something. But I missed her, too, and I wanted her back. Even if my eyes had been opened to how we weren't the best friends I'd thought we were, we'd still been friends too long to not forgive each other. And I didn't see how holding grudges was going to solve anything.

"Okay," I said. "I forgive you."

236

She smiled wide. "Thanks." There was a beat of silence, during which I busied myself trying to ease crumbs out of my keyboard with my fingernail. "So the end of the world must be coming," she said. "I'm dating someone."

"I know. I saw you two in the hall."

"Aren't you going to ask how it's going?"

And I guessed that was something I admired about Vonnie: her ability to move on. To get past weirdness and awkwardness and hard feelings. She never needed to stew over things. She never needed to pick events apart and she would never, ever hold something over someone's head. Apologize and move on. For her, life was nothing more than a series of phases. We were in the forgive-and-forget phase, and it was my choice to either play along or to fight it.

"How's it going?"

She lounged back on her elbows, stretching her legs out in front of her. "Eh. He has bad breath, and you know how I can't do bad breath. It's like letting a dog put its tongue in my mouth. So the sex is definitely not happening. Because if his breath is that bad, I can't even imagine what it must smell like when he peels his socks off."

I laughed. "Gross! But he's cute. Maybe offer him some gum or something."

She made a face. "Too much slobber. I'll probably just break up with him instead."

I shook my head. It was always so easy for Vonnie.

"What about you, Buttercup? Any men in your life right now?"

"Uh, definitely not. Maybe never again."

"Oh, please, you can't swear off men forever just because Kaleb turned out to be a superdouche."

I shut my laptop and pushed it to the side, then stretched back against my pillow. "I saw him."

Her eyes got wide and she sat up. "No way. Really? I heard he's, like, totally depressed now. I didn't want to bring it up to you, but since you saw him...how does he look?"

"He looks rough," I said. "He's changed a lot. Skinny, pale, dark circles under his eyes, that kind of thing. He apologized to me."

"For real?"

I flipped on some music and pulled a couple of magazines out of my desk drawer. I tossed one down to Vonnie, like old times. "His lawyer made him do it."

"Figures. He's a spineless weenie."

"I don't know," I said. "I think this really messed up his life."

"Good," she said. "Not to be mean or anything, but it's his own fault. What he did was really uncool."

"Yeah," I said, but I was feeling a little unsure. Yes, what Kaleb had done was his own fault, but on some level it was my own fault, too, right? I was the one who took the photo. I was the one who made that decision, and I was the one who stood in Vonnie's bathroom and took off all my clothes. And I was the one who decided to text the photo to him. Had I not done those things, he wouldn't have had the photo to send around. And it sucked for him to get that much fallout over something so foolish.

"What about you? How's community service going?" Vonnie asked.

Mack's face popped into my head. Community service had stopped being such a horrible sentence, and I guessed he was the reason why. "It's okay," I said. "There are some real interesting people in there, but there's also this guy who's pretty nice."

Vonnie perked up. "Guy?"

I shook my head. "Not like that. He's a friend. He's been my only friend for a while now."

She ducked her head. "What's he in for?"

I shut my magazine. "What's he in for? What are you, a TV cop? I don't know."

Vonnie stopped, her hand holding a page in midflip, and gazed at me. "You don't know? So he could be, like, a killer or something and you're being his friend?"

"He's not a killer. They don't sentence murderers to community service. He probably just messed up like me."

"If you say so," she singsonged. "But I'd be checking it out if I were you, Buttercup. Before I got all buddy-buddy with him. The last thing you need is another bad guy episode."

She started talking about something she'd seen on TV, and I listened to her gab for a while, my mind wandering, and then we read each other articles out of the Q&A sections in our magazines, laughing at them like we always did, and I wanted so badly for this to feel normal between us. But it didn't. People were moving on, and Vonnie had come back to me, and still I didn't feel like everything was all right. There was something missing.

"So my mom said something about a board meeting tomorrow night?" Vonnie asked.

"Yeah, I think so. I don't know much about it. My parents aren't saying a lot about that kind of stuff around me anymore."

"My mom said they were going to talk about 'the sexting issue,'" Vonnie continued, making air quotes with her fingers. "And that a couple of board members are calling for your dad to step down or be fired. Do you think he will?"

In truth, I didn't like to think about it. I didn't like to think what it would mean for our family. We couldn't live off Mom's paycheck. And what would Dad do with himself? He loved his job. He would be devastated.

"I don't know."

"It sucks. My mom says there's going to be a lot of people there. She said it would be really humiliating for your family. If I were you, I'd make sure I was nowhere near that meeting, Buttercup."

"That's probably good advice."

Vonnie stayed until we could hear Mom rattling around in the kitchen.

After she left, I wandered downstairs to see if Mom was making dinner, and I couldn't stop thinking about what

Vonnie's mom had said about the board meeting: it would be humiliating for our family.

Mom was making soup, an apron wrapped around her work clothes, her reading glasses tucked up in the nest of her graying blond hair. Her eyes looked tired, and it seemed like there were more lines around them than there used to be. I bellied up to the cutting board and began chopping the carrots she had laid out.

"Was that Vonnie?"

"Yeah. She stopped by."

"I haven't seen her in ages." Mom sounded distracted.

"We haven't really been talking all that much lately. But it's fine. We're still friends."

She glanced at me. "Well, I suppose that's good, then." She continued to stir, and I started chopping a celery stalk.

"How's work?" I asked.

"Oh, it's..." Mom said, and trailed off. She didn't turn around or ask why I was asking or do anything to make me believe she wanted to continue talking about it.

"Are people...you know...did people at your school hear about...stuff?" I scooped the celery chunks into my hands and dropped them into a bowl, then drove the knife into an onion.

She paused, and then said, "I've had a few parents upset."

"What do you mean?"

She turned and leaned her back against the stove. "Ash,

don't worry about it. They were trouble parents to begin with. The kind that complain about everything."

I put the knife down. "Upset how? What do you mean?" I repeated.

Mom closed her eyes, and I was struck with how worn down she looked, like if she stood that way for too long she'd fall asleep. Slowly she opened them again. "I've had a few parents pull their kids from the preschool. They don't think I can set a good example because of the trouble you got in. It's really not that big of a deal. We've got a waiting list to fill those spots, anyway."

I felt like I should say something. Like I should comfort Mom, or apologize. But nothing I could say could undo what had happened. It was like the fallout over what I'd done would never stop.

After a few minutes, the soup began bubbling and Mom turned to stir it again, and I went back to my chopping. I supposed we'd said everything there was to be said about the subject.

"Are you going to the board meeting tomorrow night?" I asked.

"Yes. But I'll have time to pick you up from community service and bring you home before then. That way you won't have to be there."

The board meetings were always held in the Central Office building, right upstairs from room 104, and I'd been wondering if maybe I should skip community service and come home. I definitely didn't want to be stuck in a crowd of the same people who'd said such horrible things about me online and in the media. I did not want to be there to see my dad's work, and life, become a shambles. No way.

"Do you think Dad is going to step down?"

"I don't even know if Dad knows what Dad is going to do at this point," Mom answered, and her tone told me that was all the conversation she wanted to have on the subject, so I closed my mouth.

We finished putting the ingredients into the pot; then Mom covered it and lowered the heat to let it simmer for a while. The smell was familiar and homey to me. It made me think of being a little kid, of being safe and warm and cozy, of having family dinners together with Mom and Dad, all of us talking about our days.

But I knew that now the smell was just that—a smell—and that Mom and I would exchange meaningless pleasantries over dinner, and Dad would come home late, grab a drink, and eat in stony silence. Nobody wanted to share what their day had been like because we all wanted to forget it.

As if we could.

COMMUNITY SERVICE

I was on edge when I showed up for community service the next day. The building seemed to be buzzing. A police car sat out front, which hardly ever happened, and I guessed someone had summoned the police to help keep order that night. The thought scared me a little.

Truth be told, I didn't really want to be there at all, and I almost faked a stomach flu to get me out of it. But in the end, I knew that the sooner I got through my community service, the sooner this could all be over with, and the sooner I could try to get my life back. Winter break would be coming up before long, and I had a distant hope that the time off would give everyone a chance to forget and move on to the next big scandal and that I could start a whole new semester like nothing had ever happened.

But what if they didn't? What if I remained the big topic forever? I tried not to think about the fact that I had a whole year to go after this one was done. The thought was too depressing.

I was the first one to arrive, and Mrs. Mosely looked up from her book when I walked in.

"I wasn't sure if I'd see you today or not," she said.

I placed my paper on her desk. "My mom'll take me home before the meeting starts."

Mrs. Mosely eyed me over her reading glasses and then took them off and let them hang on the chain around her neck. "Ashleigh, I think you need to know, I've never had someone come through my program with your...problem."

Great, I thought. *I'm an anomaly. And I have a problem. That makes me sound like a porn addict.* Mrs. Mosely continued. "I know a lot of kids send a lot of texts and nothing ever comes of any of it. You are not the first girl in the world to send a risqué photo of herself to her boyfriend. You know that, don't you?"

I nodded, staring down at my shoes. The conversation was beginning to get uncomfortable.

"I've had kids come through here for drugs, for assault, for all kinds of things. I had one girl come through here because she had been caught plotting to kill her mother. Can you believe that? Good student, no drugs, got in with the wrong crowd and next thing she knew she was getting arrested. A murder plot, Ashleigh. But I have never had a girl come through here because she got seen naked. I want you to know that. Your case is unusual because... it's unusual. Do you follow?"

I nodded, though I didn't really follow what she was saying at all. I already knew that my case was unusual. It didn't make me feel any better, and it didn't get me in any less trouble. And I just wanted to go to my computer and work.

"And if I were the district attorney, I might think twice about calling it anything other than unusual," she said. "Child pornography is a pretty serious label."

Didn't I know it. I often stayed up at night wondering how I would someday explain this to important people in my future. *Look, before you ask me to marry you, you should know that I distributed child porn when I was in high school....* Yuck.

Mack walked in, followed by Darrell and Angel, who were giggling over something they were looking at on Angel's cell phone.

Mrs. Mosely put her glasses back on and closed her book. "No cell phones in the room, please. You know the rule."

"But, Mose, you gotta see this. It's hilarious," Darrell said, whipping the cell out of Angel's hand and bringing it to Mrs. Mosely's desk. Even though I knew they wouldn't be stupid enough to show Mrs. Mosely the text of my photo, I still felt instant nervousness at the words "you gotta see this," as if they were. I took the opportunity to slip away.

"Hey," I said, sliding into my chair next to Mack's.

"Hey."

He navigated to whatever page he was looking for, slumped back in his seat, put his earbuds in, and began speed-clicking the mouse.

My pamphlet was almost done, and I printed out a sample copy, then slid my chair back and stood up to retrieve it from the printer. For some reason, as I passed behind Mack, a movement on his computer screen caught my eye.

"What are you...?" I asked, leaning over his shoulder to see the screen, but stopped short. Animated army guys ran around on his screen, simulated bullets flying as they aimed and shot at some incoming airplanes. "A video game?"

Mack immediately stopped clicking and leaned forward, pushing the power button on the monitor to shut it off.

"Shhh!" he hissed at me, his eyebrows twisting up into an angry knot.

"A video game?" I repeated, not really caring if anyone heard me or not. Kenzie flicked a glance over at us and then went back to whatever she was saying to Angel, shaking her head as if we were pathetic.

"Shut up, would you?" Mack said through gritted teeth.

I stood up straight, crossed my arms. It didn't make sense. We were all working, putting in our time. You didn't get out of here without having some work to show for it, so how was Mack ever going to get out if he was spending his time playing video games? "Does Mosely know? What are you going to do when it's your turn to show off the stuff you made? What are you in here for, anyway?" All the questions I'd been careful not to ask were coming out in a torrent.

He turned and looked me right in the eyes. His skin was dry and there were pimples around his hairline and his curls clung to his forehead in a clump. There was a flush on his smooth, jowly cheeks, as if he was embarrassed. "This is my business," he said in a low voice. "Step off."

"Fine," I said, and reluctantly moved toward the printer. "Don't expect me to cover for you, though. Eventually she's going to figure this out." I couldn't help wondering why she hadn't already.

He let out an angry breath and flicked his computer monitor back on.

We worked silently side by side until Mrs. Mosely cleared her throat and announced that it was time for a break. Everyone stood up and darted down the hall to stretch their legs, check their phones, do whatever it was they wished they were doing when they were in the classroom working.

I lingered behind in the hallway, watching Mack head down to the candy machine like always. I was pretty sure I was the last one he wanted to join him. Instead, I pressed my back against the wall and waited for break to be over.

"Excuse me?" a little old woman called, coming down the stairs, pressing a cane to the floor between each step. "Do you know where the board meeting is going to be held?"

Mrs. Mosely rushed over to her and grasped the woman's elbow. "I'll show you," she said, and they disappeared up the staircase, one slow step at a time.

I leaned my head back and closed my eyes. People were arriving for the board meeting. I started to feel really nervous, like they would all recognize me as I snuck out of here with Mom. Like they would all be looking at me, talking about me, gossiping about how I was probably here to do my community service for what I'd done to their poor little sons and daughters. What I'd done to them. Ridiculous.

More than anything, I wanted Vonnie to come in through the ground-floor door and be my hero. Secret me out like a movie star avoiding the paparazzi. Right now. Steal me away and whisk me to someplace where the Chesterton news didn't reach. I needed a friend.

I heard a rattle right next to my ear and my eyes flew open. Mack stood there with a box of Dots. He shook them again.

"Dots," he said.

I reached up and took it. "Thanks."

"Where'd Mosely go?"

We both tore open our boxes. I tipped a Dot into my hand; he poured a mouthful directly into his mouth. "Took some lady upstairs."

He nodded. "The board meeting."

I was surprised he knew about it. "Yeah. They plan to make my dad resign."

"He shouldn't. He didn't do anything wrong."

I sucked on the Dot, rolling it around on my tongue. "Some people would disagree with that statement. According to them, I have ruined their children forever. And he allowed it to happen. Or something like that."

"That's stupid," he said.

"I know."

Even though Mrs. Mosely hadn't gotten back yet and everyone was still hanging around in a loose circle down by the bathrooms talking and giggling, Mack and I slowly went back into the classroom, to our computers, chewing our candy.

I was moving a text box on my pamphlet when Mack turned to me.

"I'm not ordered," he said.

"Huh?"

"I didn't get court ordered to be here. So." He shrugged.

"I don't get it. What do you mean you didn't get court ordered?"

His eyes flicked toward the door, as if he was afraid someone was going to come through it and hear him. Then he lowered his eyes, and his voice. "My mom took off when I was eight. And then three months ago my dad killed himself."

"Oh," I said, my hand still stuck to my mouse. I didn't know what else to say. I wasn't even sure if I was processing his words at that point. If his mom was gone and his dad was gone, didn't that make him an orphan?

"Anyway. I didn't go into foster care, because I'm seventeen. That's why I quit school. I don't have a place. I was tardy all the time because I didn't have an alarm clock and they were going to suspend me or some shit, so I quit instead. Made it easier on everyone. Plus I hated school so it was no big loss."

"What do you mean you don't have a place? Where do you live?"

He shrugged. "Wherever I can. I've stayed at Mosely's house a few times. Friends' houses. Sometimes, if it's nice, I sleep outside. At the skate park or the creek or whatever. Places where my dad used to be."

Immediately, the image of a moonbeam illuminating the word SOLO popped into my head. Solo, as in just one. All those times I'd felt like I was so terribly alone, while my parents were fighting for me and Vonnie was checking in on me. I had no idea what "alone" really was. "That's terrible," I said.

"At first, Mosely wanted me to come here so I could write up some stuff about suicide, because I'd seen firsthand what it can do to a family. But then after I was done with that, she let me keep coming in so I could have a place to go in the afternoons. Especially when it's cold. It sucks outside when it's cold. So to answer your question, yeah, Mosely knows about the game. She doesn't mind."

"Oh," I said again, totally aware that I sounded like a fool. But I kind of figured I deserved to sound like a fool, after how much I'd been whining to him and laying all my problems on him, having no idea what his life was like. "Okay."

The rest of the group began to file in.

"Look at this. Two straight-A students getting their extra credit while the teacher's away," Kenzie said when she saw us.

"Whatever," I said.

"I'm sorry, what did you say, Supermodel? I think all the brown stuff on your nose is making you talk funny. Maybe you should take a picture of yourself and send it to everyone."

Mack turned to face her. "She said shut the fuck up. Any problems hearing that?"

Kenzie rolled her eyes. "*Pfft*, what are you, her dad? Oh, wait. No, her dad is upstairs about to get fired because his daughter is a ho."

I whipped around in my seat, but Kenzie was easing her big belly into her chair with her back to us already, and Mrs. Mosely was coming through the door. My face burned, I was so angry. And embarrassed. Here I'd just found out that Mack wasn't a criminal, and Kenzie had reminded him that I was one.

After a few minutes, Mack bumped my shoulder. "Just so you know, I got the text, too."

Of course he had. Why wouldn't he? Because he didn't go to Chesterton anymore? What did that matter? A lot of people who didn't go to Chesterton had gotten the text. Probably everyone in this room had gotten the text. Who was I kidding? It was going to be a long while before I sat in a room full of people who hadn't all seen me naked. I wanted to cry. I'd been fooling myself to think he'd been any different from anyone else.

He leaned in farther. "Back when I still had a phone. But I didn't open it up," he said.

I gazed at him.

"I never looked at the picture," he said.

And something about the earnestness in his face told me he was telling the truth. And that gave me a little, tiny glimmer of hope, that maybe there were some people out there who'd received the text and not only hadn't passed it around to their friends, or gossiped about it to everyone they knew, or uploaded it to the computer, or called me names and spread rumors about me...but flat-out hadn't looked at it at all.

Maybe those people did exist out there.

Or maybe Mack was the only one.

And I supposed that was okay, too. Because the simple fact that there was one made me feel so much better, I almost felt post-run floaty.

I finished my box of Dots just as Mom came to the classroom door. She was five minutes early, but Mrs. Mosely said she understood and wouldn't dock me the time on my sheet.

Mack took out his earbuds as I logged off and gathered my things.

"So you're not going to the meeting?" he asked.

"No way. You?"

"I don't have anywhere better to be. And I've got some stuff to print out. It could be entertaining."

I frowned. "It's not entertainment. It's my dad's job. And it's stupid, like you said." I zipped up my backpack and looped the strap over one shoulder. "I, for one, don't want to witness it."

"Come on, Ash," Mom said from the doorway. She slid the sleeve of her turtleneck up to peer at her watch.

"You could go with me," Mack said.

"I think I'll pass," I mumbled. "See you tomorrow."

I followed Mom, who turned left out of the doorway rather than right.

"I parked in back," she said, walking fast so that I had to work to keep up. "That way you don't have to go through the hall upstairs. Not that there are that many people here yet."

So Mom had done it. She'd been the friend with the getaway car on the ground floor, not Vonnie. Mom was going to secret me out of here like a movie star. Mom had been the hero I needed, without my even asking her.

"Thanks," I said, but as we hurried down the hall and out the door into the evening, I began to slow.

Mack was right. This was stupid. The whole thing—the scandal, the board meeting, the way I'd let it all define me. The cowering in corners at school, pretending I was blind and deaf and frozen and dead, the running away. The power I was giving everyone else over my life.

How long had I been letting other people decide who I was? How long had I been Kaleb's pining girlfriend? Or Vonnie's sorta best friend? Or Slut Up for Grabs? When was the last time I'd said who I was? When was the last time I'd been just Ashleigh?

Then you need to think harder....

I stopped walking.

"I want to stay," I said.

Mom turned. "What?"

"I want to stay. I want to go to the meeting."

"Oh, Ashleigh, come on, let's go. We don't have time for this. I've got to get back here in—"

"I'm not playing around, Mom. I want to go."

She took a few steps toward me, her hand still digging in the front pocket of her purse for her car keys. "Honey, I don't think you should. This is going to get ugly for your dad."

"So that's exactly why I should be there." She still looked uncertain. "Mom, I know what I'm doing. It's not going to be any tougher than anything else I've gone through since this all happened." And that part was true. Everything I'd gone through had been humiliating and embarrassing and painful and lonely, and none of it had been important. None of it had had purpose.

This was important. This had purpose.

"Please trust me," I said. "I'm fine. Frog fur." I grinned, despite the butterflies that were batting against my rib cage, making me nervous and nauseous.

Mom seemed to think it over for a few minutes, then slowly pulled her hand out of her purse. She put her arm around my shoulders, and together we walked back inside the Central Office building.

THE MEETING

Central Office didn't have a meeting room that would seat more than fifty people. Ordinarily that was not a problem. Most board meetings went entirely ignored by pretty much the whole community, so there was no need for something bigger. Dad had complained about it for years, that the community was so apathetic, it was impossible to get people to care about their kids' educations until they were ticked off about something. Judging by the crowd that was stuffing itself into the meeting room today, it looked like he had a point.

The first thing I noticed when Mom and I walked in was the TV camera. The local media had shown up. This meeting was news, I realized, and in our small community, it was big news. Mom kept her arm around my shoulders and we plowed through the people, who mostly seemed not to notice us at all, and into the back conference room, where Dad was sitting, putting together his notes.

He looked somber, hunched over a worktable with a cup of coffee in front of him. He saw Mom and me come in and started to get up.

"What's wrong?" he asked Mom.

"She wanted to come," Mom said. "I couldn't tell her no. This is about her."

"It's not," he said, his attention flicking back and forth between the two of us. "It's not about you, it's about me. You shouldn't be here. You need to let your mom take you home."

"Dad, this wouldn't even be happening if it wasn't for me. Of course it's about me. I'm fine."

His fingers trembled around the papers he was holding, and I felt a stab of worry about him. "I'm fine," I repeated, and he seemed to accept this.

We hung out in the back room until about a minute before the meeting was supposed to start. Then we headed out, Dad going to the long table where the board sat, taking his usual chair on the right-hand side of the president, and Mom taking a seat in the front row next to Dad's secretary, her chin jutting up defiantly.

I stood awkwardly in the doorway, trying not to look around much, but I couldn't help myself. People were everywhere. Every seat was full, the perimeter of the room lined with people standing, even more people spilling out into the hallway. The TV camera rolled, and I blushed and held my breath when I saw it sweep over me. I pretended I didn't know it was there, which was hard to do since it was so huge. Maybe the cameraman didn't know who I was. Maybe to them I was just a part of the crowd.

I saw Vonnie's mom and Rachel's parents and my English teacher. I saw a reporter I recognized from TV and a bunch of people I'd seen around Central Office, including Mrs. Mosely. Principal Adams was there, and some students were milling around in the back, and a couple of really old people were sitting at attention, including the woman with the cane who Mrs. Mosely had helped up the stairs.

And there, in the last row, was Mack, sitting two rows behind Mrs. Mosely, his knees propped up on the seat back in front of him. He had one earbud out and dangling down the front of his shirt. He looked curious, amused.

I didn't know him. I didn't. But I knew enough about him. I knew that he'd lost far more in his life than I probably ever would in mine. I knew that he wasn't whining about it, he wasn't cowering or raging or blaming. He was moving on, doing his thing, keeping going.

And I also knew that he'd gotten the text, but he hadn't looked, and somehow that was all I needed to know about him. He hadn't looked.

I made my way to the last row and sat next to him. He acknowledged me by tipping a box of Tic Tacs into my palm.

The meeting started out pretty slow. The secretary read

the minutes; they went over some budget issues, talked about some textbook changes they wanted to make for next year. People shifted uncomfortably in their seats, crossing and uncrossing their legs while they waited for the board to get to the reason they were all there—the juicy stuff.

Finally the board president called for new business.

"Of course," he said, gazing down at the sheet of paper in front of him, "there's the matter of the, uh, call for the resignation of Superintendent Maynard for the, uh, mishandling of the, uh, texting issue at Chesterton High School. We'll open the floor for comments."

Mishandling? What did he mean by mishandling? Dad had confiscated phones, he'd contacted the police, and he—my own dad—had agreed to having me suspended from school. How else could he have handled it? This smelled like a setup to me. The president wanted Dad gone, and that was all there was to it.

A woman came up to the microphone and straightened her sweater. She leaned forward like she thought her mouth needed to be right on the microphone for her to be heard. The result was that all of her "P"s and "T"s and "S"s blew thunderously into our ears.

"My daughter goes to Chesterton High School," she began, "and even though she didn't receive the text, she was shown the photo by one of the boys in her class...."

My hands balled into fists as I listened to her talk about how damaged her daughter had been by the photo, and I could feel my shoulders begin to ache with tension. After she was done speaking, another woman stood up, and then a man after her. Everyone somehow claimed to be a victim of what I'd done, and everyone was blaming Dad.

As the fourth person stood and ambled toward the microphone, Mack bumped my shoulder with his.

"Let's get out of here," he whispered.

I shook my head. "I need to be here."

"I've got something we can do, though," he said, and he leaned over to one side and picked up a rolled bunch of papers from the floor.

He unrolled one. It was a small poster. A poster made from the photo I'd taken for my pamphlet, with the shot of the pillow front and center: A PICTURE'S WORTH A THOUSAND WORDS.

Only he'd changed it. Off to the side of the pillow he'd added: BUT THEY DON'T TELL THE WHOLE STORY.

I blinked and reread it a few times, a smile curving my lips upward. It was perfect.

He reached into his jean jacket pocket and pulled out two rolls of tape, then offered one to me. I took it.

Together, we stood up and, ignoring the crowd as they turned in their seats to look at us curiously, we began edging behind and around people and taping the posters to the walls.

"Young man," the board president said, after it became clear that everyone was getting restless. "Young man, you may not disrupt this meeting...."

But we ignored him, too, hanging up one more, slapping on pieces of tape as voices began to murmur around us, and then rushing out of the boardroom, laughing. My hands were shaking, but I felt great.

"Thank you for this," I said, and we turned and taped two each on the meeting room's doors before going outside to place folded copies under as many windshield wipers as we could in the parking lot. Then we sat on the bench and waited for the meeting to adjourn, Mack's earbuds stretched between us, his fedora perched jauntily on top of his head.

Eventually, people began filing out of the building, some of them glaring at us, some looking amused. Mom and Dad were the last out of the building, their arms looped together as they walked. The board had taken a vote and decided, not unanimously, not to take further action at this time. Dad had never taken his resignation speech out of his sport coat pocket. He would not resign. At least not today. Not over this.

COMMUNITY SERVICE

I bought my lunch. For the first time since the day I threw my pudding cup in the trash bin, I bought, and ate, lunch at my old table with my head up. A turkey sandwich, French fries, a brownie, chocolate milk. Like an elementary school kid.

A group of girls had called me a slut when they walked by my locker earlier in the day, and I didn't know if it was the school board meeting the night before, or the posters, or the ice cream sundaes my dad had made to celebrate afterward, but suddenly I was just done. Done being everyone's victim.

"Hey," I called to their backs. They turned around. They were wearing snotty sneers on their faces, rolling their eyes as if it physically pained them to have to look at me. "You can call me whatever you want. It's not going to bother me anymore. But if calling me a slut makes you feel better about yourselves, then you should probably look into that, because you have a problem."

They didn't respond. Just shook their heads at me and marched off, whispering to each other. But I didn't care. I felt triumphant anyway, and I had decided I was sick of being hungry because I was too afraid to eat lunch.

I took my tray to the cashier and punched in my ID number to pay, then stood in the doorway of the cafeteria looking in.

At first my brain saw it the way it had been for me for weeks now: frightening, cold, lonely. But I reminded myself that if I could hang posters at the board meeting last night, I could do anything. If I could call out those girls in the hallway, I could sit at a lunch table. I could take my life back. So I did.

I marched over to my old table, where Vonnie, Cheyenne, and Annie were all sitting. I pasted a smile on my face and sat down.

"Hey, Buttercup," Vonnie said, pulling a bag of chips out of her Hello Kitty lunch bag.

"Hey," I said, and I made sure I made eye contact with all three of them. I wanted Cheyenne and Annie to know that I was taking my space back, whether they liked it or not. I was done hiding, and if they couldn't handle what that did to their precious reputations, that was their problem.

Cheyenne smiled. "Hi, Ash." Annie followed with a smile of her own.

That was all it took.

I sat down and dug into my food, thinking it was the best meal I'd ever eaten in my whole life, and we chatted about school and homework and who was wearing what to the winter formal. Nobody brought up texts or naked photos or Kaleb or community service.

After a while, Rachel came to the table and stood over Cheyenne's shoulder, a sour look on her face. She had to wait a few minutes before everyone noticed her.

"You're not supposed to be sitting here," she said.

I swallowed my bite of sandwich. "Actually, *you're* not supposed to be here. I was here first, which means you have to stay away."

She cocked her head to one side, like I was some kind of imbecile. "I sit here every day and you know it."

I sipped my milk. "But today I got here first, which means you have to find somewhere else to sit. Which is what I've been doing. Only I've been doing it with a lot less drama."

"Von? For real?" Rachel whined, putting one hand on her hip like she was challenging Vonnie to kick me out. I held my breath, waiting to see what Vonnie's response was going to be. I kept my food in midchew, not daring to swallow. Vonnie had told me she was going to stop hanging around with Rachel. This would be the real test of our friendship. If Vonnie chose Rachel, I was done with her.

"I'm sitting with Ashleigh," Vonnie said, and Cheyenne and Annie nodded in agreement. I swallowed, breathed.

Rachel squinted at Vonnie's back, a look of total hatred,

and then huffed. "Whatever," she mumbled, and turned her back on us as she scanned the cafeteria for somewhere else to sit.

A part of me felt victorious. I'd won a small battle. My friends had stood behind me in their own tentative way. And if they hadn't, I'd been prepared to go find better friends. I was owning my existence. Maybe for the first time ever.

Vonnie and the girls went back to their lunch and chit-chat, but I zoned most of it out, only adding to the conversation when someone asked me something specific. Mostly I thought about Rachel. About what had happened between us. It needed resolving.

When the bell rang, we all sprang up out of our chairs. I dumped the garbage and set my tray on the conveyor belt, and then turned and peered through the crowd for Rachel.

I finally found her, leaving the cafeteria with a couple of girls I didn't know. She turned the corner and I followed her, catching up with her as she reached her locker.

"Rachel," I said.

She turned, her face going from curious to disgusted instantly. "What is your deal?" she said. "You're supposed to stay away from me."

"For my protection, Rachel, not yours. Remember? I didn't do anything to you. It was the other way around. But it doesn't matter now. I think we need to talk."

She leaned back against her closed locker. The girl at the locker next to her tried to look nonchalant, but it was totally obvious that she was listening to us. "What do we need to talk about?" Rachel asked in a bored voice.

I took a deep breath. "I don't ever want to be your friend again, but I think it'll be impossible for us to always avoid each other. So I know it's in the court order that you have to stay away from me, but I honestly don't care if you don't."

She rolled her eyes. "Oh, so you're all bigger than me now, is that it?"

"No, but... what you did really messed up my life. And I thought we were friends, which made it even worse. I still don't know why you did it. But I'm sick of thinking about it. I'm sick of my life being about that picture. So if you come around, I won't make a big deal out of it. I want life to get back to normal. I'll just... ignore you." I couldn't offer her friendship, but this seemed like the closest I could come to it.

The girl next to us finally shut her locker and moved on. The crowd in the hallway was getting thinner; soon it would just be the two of us standing there. I noticed Mr. Green, the French teacher, standing in his doorway eyeing us warily, as if he expected a fight to break out.

"It was supposed to be a joke," Rachel said. "I wasn't trying to be mean."

"Well, it wasn't funny," I said. "But I'm over it now. What you say or do doesn't matter to me anymore."

I turned and walked away from her, and it felt so good to leave her back there, leave her with the understanding that I didn't need a court order to keep her out of my life. Leave her with the knowledge that no matter what "joke" she played on me, I would come out on top. Fighting Rachel only spurred her on. Telling her that she didn't matter—and really meaning it—was the best way to disarm her.

She wouldn't give me any grief anymore.

I was a long way from peace, but I was at least one step closer.

After school, I told Mack all about what had happened, as we walked around the building taking down the posters, per Mosely's orders. He laughed out loud when I told him about the look on Rachel's face when she realized I wasn't going to kiss her ass anymore.

When we were done, we went back to room 104 and straight to our computers. I only had a few hours left to finish my pamphlet. My community service was almost complete.

But before I got to work, I rolled up a few of the posters and slipped them into my backpack. I planned to hang them in my bedroom. My time in room 104 was about to end, but I didn't want to forget it. Not all of it.

LAST DAY

COMMUNITY SERVICE

Mrs. Mosely brought in pizza for my graduation day.

I stood up in front of the semicircle of chairs, my stomach growling for some pepperoni.

Kenzie's seat was empty because she'd gone into labor the night before. Nobody knew if she'd had her baby yet or not, even though Angel kept texting her to find out. Kenzie never answered the texts, which led us to all speculate on whether that meant she was in labor at that moment, and we all joked about how we felt sorry for the nurses who had to deal with Kenzie in pain.

Kenzie would have to finish her community service after she got out of the hospital, but by then I would be gone, and I would probably never find out whether she'd had a boy or a girl. Not that it mattered. I doubted our paths would cross again. At least I hoped they wouldn't.

We'd gotten two new people in Teens Talking. One was a girl who was only twelve and had gotten busted for running away from home too many times. Another was a boy who'd broken his mom's arm for trying to take away his car keys. Neither of them went to Chesterton High, but both of them knew why I was there. But I found that I didn't care about that as much as I used to. People talked. Let them talk. Nothing I could do to stop them. They knew the thousand words, but they didn't know the rest of the story.

And of course Mack was still there. I'd brought him a whole bagful of candy as a good-bye present.

Mrs. Mosely gave her usual speech about being respectful and listening to my presentation, and then I got up and talked about the events that had led to me being there.

Finally, I opened my pamphlet, which was packed with facts about sexting, and held it face-out so everyone could see.

"Studies show that one in five students ages twelve to seventeen have sent or received nude photos via text," I began, and I found that as I talked, I was a lot less mortified about what had happened to me. I wasn't alone. It wasn't just me. Others had gone through what I'd gone through, and some of them had come out okay. Maybe I would, too. In fact, maybe I would come out more okay than some of the others who'd sent my photo to their friends to be cruel.

Because you can get past a mistake, but it's much harder to get past being a cruel person.

I read all the facts in my pamphlet. I was proud of the work I'd put into it. I hoped it would help someone not get into the mess I'd gotten into. And I'd shown off Mack's poster, because I was proud of it, too.

When I was finished, Mrs. Mosely told us we could take a pizza break. I grabbed a paper plate and piled a couple of slices on it, and then headed to my usual spot at the computer next to Mack's. Only this time, as I munched, I didn't have anything to work on.

I pulled up the same video game Mack was using and started playing.

"You glad to get out of here?" he asked, sliding into his chair, holding a plate piled high with pizza slices.

"Yes. Definitely." I threw a grenade.

"What are you gonna do with your time now?" he said.

"Besides school? Run, I think," I said. "I miss it. I thought I wouldn't, because I wasn't running with Kaleb anymore, but it turns out I like to run. I won't miss him."

And that was the truth. As much as at one point I'd felt like I would die if he was seeing someone else, I didn't even think about him most days anymore. I hated that his life had been so messed up by what had happened, and I believed he was sorry. But what happened to him wasn't about me anymore. We were broken up, and I had moved on, and that was all that mattered.

Mrs. Mosely got busy helping one of the new kids with

research, and everyone went back to work, their greasy pizza fingers leaving little wet swipes on the keyboards.

Except for Mack and me. We slouched down until we were comfortable in our chairs. We stretched an earbud cord between us and both jammed out while playing a video game. After our pizza was gone, he opened the bag of candy I'd brought him and we both dipped into that as well, filling our bellies with chocolate and sugar.

When our time was up, we filed out like any other day, only this time I wouldn't be coming back, and that seemed really weird to me.

Dad was waiting for me inside the doors, his overcoat buttoned up to the top and a scarf wrapped around his neck. It was finally getting cold outside, and I could see Mack's breath puff out in front of him as he traipsed along the sidewalk.

I paused and turned to Dad. "I think I'll walk home today," I said.

His eyebrows went up in surprise. "It's freezing out there."

"I'll run some of it," I said. "Plus I've got my coat. I'll be fine."

Dad shrugged and pushed open the doors. He walked toward his car, and I jogged up next to Mack.

"I'm coming with you," I said, bringing my knees up high to my belly with each jogged step to keep warm. "Skate park?"

He nodded. "Okay."

We didn't spend much time on the ramps at all. It was too cold. But that was okay with me, because what I really wanted was to go back into the creek. I had something to take care of.

I led the way, Mack silently trundling along behind me. It was surprisingly warm inside the tunnel, and now I understood why Mack sometimes slept there, especially when it was dry. Our footsteps echoed off the walls like before, only this time they had more purpose to them. I walked right toward the rectangles of light and turned to face the tag wall.

"I brought something," I said. I opened my backpack and pulled out a small can of silver spray paint that I'd gotten out of my garage that morning.

Mack didn't say anything, just grinned, his skin cold and tight under that greasy mop of bangs, and watched as I shook the can and pulled off the lid.

I crouched to find an empty space right next to Solo and poised my finger over the trigger. I knew exactly what I was going to write. I was not just Kaleb's pining girlfriend. I was not just Vonnie's bestie. I was not just a cross-country runner. I was definitely not Slut Up for Grabs.

I was not my mistakes. I was not defined by anyone else. Only I got to say who I was.

And I was ... me.

Just Ashleigh.

I pressed the trigger and drew a big, loopy, celebratory "A."

ACKNOWLEDGMENTS

Items found in the Thousand Words Thrift Store of Novel-Writing Appreciation (and their stories):

A pair of ginormous, glittery pom-poms, a soft handkerchief, and a set of crutches: Belonging to my agent, Cori Deyoe, whose unrelenting support and encouragement never fail to see me through.

A spelunking headlamp and a safety line: Owned by my editor, Julie Scheina, whose revisions helped me mine a story, bring it up to the surface, and see it in a much fuller, deeper light. A bundle of bright red pencils and a pair of X-ray goggles: A gift from Pam Garfinkel, who answers questions, offers opinions, and makes suggestions like nobody's business. **A worn and well-loved dictionary:** Property of Barbara Bakowski and Barbara Perry, who never cease to amaze me with their command of the English language and attention to detail. **And an artist's smock:** From Erin McMahon and her beautiful design work.

A rubber chicken and a bottle of bubble bath: Removed from the closet of Susan Vollenweider, the first person to read chapter 1 and encourage me to keep going, but, more important, the person who listens the most, who makes me laugh, and who resists the urge to throw things at my head when I get whiny. **A doctor's kit:** Once belonging to Rhonda Stapleton, who dropped everything to read and make suggestions on chapter headings. **A cozy bathrobe:** The tag inside the collar reads MICHELLE ZINK, the lovingest and most supportiest author I know.

A clock with no hands and no batteries, and a teddy bear for snuggling: Donated by my children, who are so patient with my divided time and the sharing of the laptop. You are all Mommy's favorite.

A big box of...awesome: A gift from my husband, Scott, who does nothing but provide boundless support, ideas, troubleshooting, research articles, contacts, hugs, and, most important, belief. I love you.

Thank you to all of you!

I was a teen in the 1980s. We had no cell phones. No laptops or social networking, no Skype, texting, or instant messaging. Our cameras were 110 point-and-shoots, which turned out grainy photos that took about a week to get developed, unless you were loaded enough to afford the fancy-schmancy one-hour processing.

In so many ways, we were less instantly connected, forced to rely on passing paper notes in class and waiting—sometimes hours or even days—for our friends to write back. Having to call friends while tethered to the kitchen wall by a curly phone cord (that our hair always, always got tangled in). And every snapshot we took was gandered at by the film developer. In fact, the film-developing shop at my local mall dropped the finished photos, one by one, off a conveyor belt into a window on the outside of the shop, so everyone who walked by could stare at our business.

Before the days of camera phones and texting, if we fretted about being caught naked by our peers, what we feared was a terrifying Public Nudity Accident, such as the classic Showing Up Naked in Algebra Class nightmare coming true, or a Great Bikini Elastic Disaster occurring at the municipal pool.

But that's not to say we didn't get naked in front of people we maybe shouldn't have. Of course we did. The 1980s may seem like prehistoric times, but we were still human. And humans get naked. Humans experiment with things like sex and do dumb things like take on ridiculous dares or make bad decisions to show off or to get attention or as a joke, or sometimes for no reason at all.

And because we were human, we messed up, and certainly there were negative consequences to some of our more naked decisions. Some consequences were worse than others—embarrassment, ridicule, grounding, arrest. Just like experimentation and poor decision making, all those unfortunate penalties existed before sexting, too.

Recent statistics say that 20 percent of teens have sent nude or seminude photos or videos of themselves to someone else. That's a lot of nakedness floating around out there in cyberspace, just waiting to be seen by the wrong eyes.

Just waiting for an accident or a joke or a bully or a revenge plot. Just waiting to be passed around.

But whether or not you've ever had a nude episode in your life, we've all had our moments of feeling awfully exposed in front of our peers. We've all had our moments of being...bare.

Nobody wants to be in a "bare" situation. Nobody wants a naked body—or a naked soul, for that matter—to be out there for the world to see, to judge, to comment on. We want to keep our most private parts covered, whether they be internal parts or external ones. We want to decide when and how and to whom we are exposed.

But if we find ourselves in a naked situation, in 1983 or 2013, literally or figuratively, how we handle the fallout is what matters most. There's nothing you can do to take back that naked moment, that nude text. There's no way to turn back time so you can cover up and keep it covered. But there's plenty of time to learn how to move forward. As Bea told Valerie in my first novel, *Hate List*, "Just like there's always time for pain, there's always time for healing."

Do we let the people with the judgmental comments and the quick Send finger take us down emotionally? Do we let those intent on hurting us define us? Do we let them get to say who we are, just because they think they know us, based on one bare moment?

Or do we, like Mack, remind ourselves that our unveilers know only part of the story, know only part of who we really are? And do we, like Ashleigh, ultimately take back ourselves, because no matter how naked we get, one bad decision does not an identity make?

Ultimately, it is up to us how bare we want to be in front of the world. And it always has been.

Technology aside.

WITH JENNIFER BROWN

WHAT MADE YOU WANT TO WRITE THIS STORY?

As with all my books, I wanted to write it because it's relevant. There are teens out there who are experiencing the humiliation and embarrassment that Ashleigh goes through, simply by virtue of making a poor decision. A lot of teens who need to hear that they're not alone.

I spent much time during my teen years feeling isolated, so it's important to me to reach out to teens in pain, to let them know that there is a light at the end of this tunnel they're going through and that things will get better for them. I don't have answers, but if I can create a character readers can relate to and then give that character hope, and in turn give the reader hope, I'm happy.

WHAT HAPPENS TO ASHLEIGH AND KALEB IS PRETTY SCARY. CAN THAT REALLY HAPPEN?

Can and has! While several states have changed, or are currently working to change, laws surrounding teen sexting, in some states sending a nude photo of a teen is considered distribution of child pornography, a felony offense. Teens and young adults could find themselves arrested, charged, convicted, ordered to do community service or other diversion programs, or even given jail time and required to register as a sex offender.

But there are a great many more cases of teens who've had to deal with emotional fallout of sexting gone awry. There are cases in which teens have had their nude texts go viral, have found themselves ridiculed to the point of having to move to a new school, have been suspended. And, sadly, there are even instances of teens committing suicide as a result of bullying due to nude texts.

That's why it's so important to think before you hit Send. Anything you send out into cyberspace is out there forever. You can't take it back, and you never know when you might sorely want to.

WHY DOES KALEB DO SOMETHING SO MEAN TO ASHLEIGH?

Revenge, plain and simple. He is angry with Ashleigh and wants to get back at her for what he thinks she did to him. His thinking is short-term, as we so often tend to be guilty of when we're angry, and he doesn't realize the lasting effects his actions might have. He doesn't think about how quickly or how far things can spread; nor does he think about the trouble he can get himself into. Whether or not he intends for Ashleigh to be as humiliated as she is (certainly, he wants her to experience *some* humiliation), he definitely doesn't intend to put himself in the line of fire like that.

WHY DON'T VONNIE AND CHEYENNE AND ANNIE STAND BY ASHLEIGH WHEN SHE GETS INTO TROUBLE?

Vonnie and Cheyenne and Annie aren't sure how to deal with all the fallout. Vonnie feels guilty for her own part in what happened, but she also believes that it isn't the huge deal Ashleigh is making it out to be. Vonnie thinks it will all blow over eventually, and in the meantime she wants to distance herself from it so she won't get any fallout of her own.

Plus, Ashleigh is suspended, so for weeks the others are at school without her, their lives going on, and eventually they just kind of...drift apart.

But they don't turn away from her in a sense that they will never be friends again. Everyone just needs some space and time. I think that's important to remember, too. Grudges benefit nobody, and a little time to think may be all that's needed to repair a wounded relationship.

YOUR STORIES ARE SO SERIOUS. DO YOU THINK YOU'LL EVER WRITE A COMEDY?

I actually can write comedy, and in fact wrote a humor column for the *Kansas City Star* for more than four years. However, comedy writing, while easier for me than "serious" writing, was never comfortable for me. I have been quite happy to leave it behind. So at the moment I have no immediate plans to write comedy—especially YA comedy—but you never know what the future holds.

MANY OF YOUR BOOKS FOCUS ON A BOYFRIEND-GIRLFRIEND RELATIONSHIP GONE BAD. WHY?

Because these are the relationships that I remember most vividly from when I was a teen. Best-friend and boyfriend relationship problems caused me so much pain and angst! So a part of me may be still trying to work out relationships-gone-sour circa the 1980s, but also a part of me knows that I was definitely not alone. Boyfriend-girlfriend relationships cause angst for everyone! The complexity of relationships, in general, intrigues me. There's so much to talk about. I could write a thousand books and never touch on it all.